The Zoo Crew

Dustin Stevens

The Zoo Crew

For Pop.

I'm in love with Montana. For other states I have admiration, respect, recognition, even some affection. But with Montana it is love. And it's difficult to analyze love when you're in it.

– John Steinbeck

Prologue

Missoula, Montana.

Fifteen thousand years ago the entire region was buried beneath five hundred cubic miles of glacial runoff. The Salish Indians, one of a handful of tribes that called the area home, named it *nmesuletk.*

The place of frozen water.

Two thousand years ago, after the water dried up, the first European settlers drifted into the area and stole the land and the name. Translated into English it became Missoula, a name it has held for over three hundred years since.

Despite its official title, over time the town has born many monikers.

To the hippies that arrive in droves every year seeking low cost of living and the highest marijuana use per capita in the country, it's MisSOULa.

To the advertising executives trying to make a buck on the pristine beauty of Western Montana, it's the gateway to Glacier and Yellowstone National Parks.

To the Chamber of Commerce it's the Garden City, a rather odd name for a city that's lucky to see four months of growing season each year.

But to the locals, both native and adopted, Missoula is simply The Zoo.

And what a zoo it is.

Chapter One

Pain.

Pleasure.

Two fundamentally opposed sensations that at their most basic levels have a great deal in common.

Both can render a person speechless. Both can leave the mind blank. Both can overwhelm the senses to the point of exhausted numbness.

For most people, it is an either/or scenario. They've either been injured or are in a state of complete bliss. No middle ground.

Notch, though, is not most people. He has made a career out of mixing pain and pleasure. If he were a bartender, he would be world renowned for inventing concoctions. Elixirs that left people flat on their back, unable to move.

The secret ingredient? Other people's pain is his pleasure.

"You see ladies," Notch hissed, his voice barely discernible, "the key is to clip the vocal chords first. That way no matter how much she screams and thrashes about, we don't have to listen to it. Kind of like watching a television with the sound off."

As he spoke, he walked a small circle around his prey. Her hands were tied high above her head. A leather thong bound them together and disappeared into the rafters above.

Blood and sweat ran down her arms. Thick tendrils of both striped her blonde hair.

An ugly smear stretched across her throat where he had clipped her vocal chords. Seared the wound shut with a heated knife blade.

Her dirty feet hung several inches above the floor. Kicked in vain for the ground beneath her.

She was completely naked.

An unwilling audience sat just inches away from her.

Seated on the floor in a semi-circle was a half dozen girls. None far into their twenties. All in some stage of pregnancy.

Every face was ashen and tear stained. All looked like they might throw up at any moment.

"See, now that we've hit the mute button, we can have some fun," Notch said.

With one hand he grabbed the girl by the hip. Spun her in a clockwise direction until the leather thong binding her was wound tight. Hefted his blade up next to her. Released his grip, letting the tension spin her around.

As the thong did its job, he pressed the tip of the knife against her skin. Lowered it the length of her body.

Bright red droplets spattered the concrete beneath her as a serpentine line striped her skin. Trails of blood seeped down from the line.

Notch waited until she stopped spinning and smiled down at the girls seated on the floor. "I like to call that one the Candy Cane."

Every last one of them tried to avert their eyes. Tears stained their already puffy cheeks.

Tethered beside him, the girl continued to throw her head back in agony. No sound came out.

His orders had been simple enough.

Find the girl. Bring her to this address. Make an example of her.

Her pain, his pleasure.

Notch waited to make sure the effect found its mark. Dropped the knife and picked up a pair of pliers. "Apparently our little friend here has been doing some talking, trying to go back on her agreement."

He held the pliers out in front of him and asked, "Do you all know what happens when you go back on your agreement?"

In one quick movement, he thrust the pliers forward. Clamped them onto the girl's front teeth. Twisted them up at a ninety degree angle, snapping the teeth off at the gum line.

"You get punished," Notch said. Opened the pliers and let the teeth drop to the cement.

The girls in front of him, the ones that weren't already vomiting or trying to crawl away, recoiled in horror.

He knew he was on the verge of losing them. It was time for a big finish.

"I hope, for your sakes, that this is the last time we meet," Notch said. Swapped out the pliers for the knife. "But if it isn't..."

One wicked slash of the razor-honed blade was all it took. The thin white skin of the girl's abdomen gave no resistance. The steel carved her stomach like a jack-o-lantern.

Over twenty feet of intestine smacked against the ground with a wet slap.

Three of the girls on the floor wrenched out every bit of food left in their system. The other three keeled straight back, passed out from shock.

Notch never said another word. He didn't have to. He had been told to make an example of her. He had done that.

His money would be waiting on him when he left, a fact that made him smirk every time he thought about it.

He would do this kind of work for free, no questions asked.

Their pain, his pleasure.

Chapter Two

First day.

Of September. Of the third year of law school.

Of the reconvening of the Zoo Crew.

Drake Bell was the first to arrive. He always was. The high beams from his truck cut a swath through the empty parking lot. Stared a hole through the pine trees in front of him as he left the truck running and waited for the others.

After three months back home in Tennessee, he could not get the cab of the truck warm enough. He was a southern boy through and through. Despite the past seven years spent in Missoula, he still wasn't used to the cold.

Doubted he ever would be.

Not that he could even pretend that September 1st was cold. More like crisp.

Drake was just a few hours back in Missoula after a summer spent interning for the Innocence Project in Nashville. He'd hated every second of it.

The humidity was atrocious, the cost of living outrageous. The work was tedious and the people insufferable.

The reason he'd taken the position was threefold. First, a professor had gone out on a limb to set it up for him. He hadn't asked her to and had no interest in death row work. After she'd gone to the trouble though, he couldn't very well say no.

Second, standing on the edge of his third year in law school, he needed something that resembled legal experience. Even if it was just enough to tell him to stay far, far away from all things judicial.

Third, and most important, he had to go back and deal with what he'd been putting off for three years.

Nashville was no longer home to him, hadn't been in a while. He just told people that because it explained his accent and, well, he had to be from somewhere. At least Nashville seemed to get a favorable response from folks.

After this summer though, Drake doubted he'd ever go back. To visit, let alone live.

Sage was the second to show up, just like always. Drake recognized her by the low twin lights of her Honda Civic. They swung into the parking lot and slid in on the far side of his truck. He made no effort to get out as the lights blacked out and his passenger side door was wrenched open.

"Hey stranger," Sage said. Climbed in and slammed the door shut. "When'd you get in?"

Drake rubbed his hands over his face. A two day beard scraped against his palms. "Either late last night or early this morning. Not sure which."

"I was wondering if you'd make it this morning."

A wry smile tugged at Drake's face. "You weren't wondering anything. You just hoped I'd be late so you could give me shit about it."

Sage's white teeth stared back at him through the darkened cab. "Can't blame a girl for trying. You think it's warm enough in here?"

"Not really."

"You went south and got soft on us didn't you?"

A single headlight appeared through the darkness and turned into the parking lot. Drake watched as it wound down the opposite side and came to a stop facing the truck. Its driver was little more than a shadow as he climbed off and nodded at the truck.

"I would have bet money Ajax was done with that motorcycle by now," Drake said.

Sage snorted. "This may be the third time he's rode it all summer. He's just on it now to make a point to you."

"I'm touched," Drake said. Overhead, the first grey streaks of light started to split the sky. "Your brother back or is it just the three of us today?"

"Said he'll be here," Sage said. "But who knows."

In front of them, the silhouette of Ajax pulled his helmet off and balanced it on the seat.

"Naw, if he said he'll be here, he'll be here," Drake said. "You know the rules in Montana."

"Yeah, I know," Sage groaned. "Church, work, and fishing. But you also know the rules for a firefighter just getting back from a busy season."

"Desperado's or Blue's?" Drake asked.

"Despo's."

"He'll be here," Drake said and turned off the engine. He killed the headlights and together they emerged from the truck. The morning air was frigid after the warmth of the cab.

They made no effort to unload anything from the bed, instead circling around to the front.

"We'll if it's not the swinging dick of Montana Law himself," Ajax said, coming halfway to greet them. He extended a closed fist to Drake. Drake matched it, followed by a shoulder hug.

"In the flesh," Drake said, clapping his friend on the back.

Ajax was the Zoo Crew's given nickname for Adam Jackson, Drake's roommate since freshmen year of undergrad at the University of Montana. A trust fund kid from Boston, the only reason he'd chosen UM was because it was three thousand miles away.

No chance of his family ever stopping by for a visit.

In six years, Drake had met them one time. It was graduation, and they all looked miserable for every second of it. Of course, in a state as white as Montana, that's not surprising.

The running joke was that Ajax was the only black guy in the state that wasn't there to play sports.

"How's my girl doing?" Drake asked.

Ajax made a face and looked to Sage. "You believe this guy? Been gone two months and the first thing he does is ask how his dog's doing."

Sage broke into a smile and raised her hands. "I want no part of this."

"Damn dog is dead," Ajax spat. "I cooked her and ate her the day you left."

Drake smiled. "Thanks for watching her for me. Appreciate it."

"Yeah, I still don't know why you couldn't just take the damn thing with you. Tennessee ain't that far."

Drake made no effort to respond. Instead he cocked an ear to the wind and listened as the oversized muffler on a Dodge Ram rumbled in the distance. Soon the other two picked it up as well.

All three took up posts around the front of Drake's truck and waited as the sound materialized into a final pair of headlights outlined by a string of orange parking lights. They remained leaning against the cold metal as the new arrival rolled to a crooked stop.

The passenger door burst open and a disheveled mess of a man spilled from it. The smell of booze came with him.

"Hey," Kade said, staggering towards them. "I'm not late am I?"

The three all smiled broadly in the early morning light and hung their heads above the hood of Drake's truck.

It had been a long ass summer, but at last the Zoo Crew was back together again.

Chapter Three

The Zoo Crew.

Never a bigger bunch of misfits had the world ever seen.

Not the world of Western Montana anyway.

To the left of the hood, just past the driver's side door, was Drake. A couple of inches above six feet tall and a dozen pounds north of two hundred, he looked at least somewhat like the norm in lily-white Missoula.

Blonde hair cropped close to his scalp. Blue eyes. A perpetual two day beard. Arms and chest that insinuated he could still play for the Grizzlies if called into action.

It was, after all, the Griz that had pulled him out from Tennessee to begin with.

Beside him, elbows pressed against the front the grill, was Ajax. He had a couple of inches on Drake, though he weighed maybe a hundred fifty pounds on a good day. Soaking wet. Before he went to the bathroom.

His entire structure was little more than bone and sinew with smooth caramel colored skin stretched taut across it. Every blood vessel and muscle striation on his body was plainly evident for the world to see.

Despite the seven figure trust fund somewhere in Boston with his name on it, he'd never touched a cent. A world class gamer, he'd made more than twice that designing software from the living room of the home he shared with Drake.

Not that a soul in Missoula outside the Zoo Crew had any idea.

On the passenger side of the hood stood Sage Keuhl, her brother Kade leaning against her. They were the most local of the Crew, having matriculated sixty miles south from Ronan to Missoula.

A little over an hour by car. Light years in just about every other way.

Located in the dead center of the Flathead Indian Reservation, Ronan was the anti-Missoula. The town knew it, and made sure everybody else did too.

Kade was the first of the two to make the trip down. Even at eighteen he knew the best way for him to go to college was to offer up his body to the football gods.

When the Griz came calling, he went running.

And tackling.

And intercepting passes.

Drake played outside linebacker, Kade played free safety. Both were outliers of a sort on the team, one from the South and another from the rez. They became friends out of necessity, stayed that way by choice.

After graduation, Kade became a forest firefighter with the Fire Boys out of Lolo. Extreme athleticism and a wanton disregard for his physical well-being made him a natural at it.

Four months out of the year he went all over the west throwing himself at anything that burned. The rest of the year he was in Missoula, throwing himself at anything in a skirt.

Not a bad life, by any metric.

Beside him was Sage, the most recent addition to the Crew. A more befitting name on someone there never was, always doling out her own brand of wisdom to others. Such advice came free of charge and was given whether it was sought out or not.

Two years younger than the other three, she shot past Missoula to Bozeman for nursing school. After three years on the other side of the state, she fled the new money and pretention of Bozo and ran back west. She was now starting her third year as an RN at Saint Michael's Hospital on the north side of town.

Through undergrad, Sage had simply been known as Kade's sister. Once she returned to Missoula and started running with the Crew, it didn't take long for her to develop an identity of her own.

Now she was as indispensible to the Crew as any other member.

The offspring of a German father and a Kootenai mother, the siblings looked like an odd mash of genetic material. Both had the long dark hair and pointed features of their Native American mother. The light skin and blue eyes of their father.

Kade was two inches shorter than six feet with a wiry build from a lifetime of handling a chainsaw and fighting fires. Sage was a couple of inches shorter than him, everything about her graceful and lithe.

Faced with the same dilemma as many mixed-race children across the country, they found themselves too white for the rez and too brown for Missoula.

Instead, they found the Zoo Crew, who could care less if they were purple.

They were, as Drake often pointed out, the Keuhl Kids.

The Crew had started in the spring of their freshmen year. It began as a joke, an excuse for the three of them to blow off studying for finals as long as possible.

Three days a week, more if their schedules allowed it, they convened in the morning hours for some outdoor recreation. In the spring and summer it was fishing. In the winter, skiing. Filling in the gaps was hiking, snowshoeing, rafting, whatever was available.

Get up and get outside. That was the only rule.

During the fall they let up some to accommodate football season. Same for exam period. Otherwise, it didn't matter how late one got in, or even if they got in at all, they made it to the Zoo Crew.

"I would hug you right now, but I don't trust myself to walk over there," Kade said. His words were slurred. He didn't care.

"And you're waiting to only see one of me?" Drake asked.

"Hey, there are three right now," Kade said. "That's better than an hour ago."

Ajax leaned back from the hood and looked over at Kade's truck. "Do we even wanna know what low-level, crab-infested, bus stop skank is driving over there?"

Sage snorted out a laugh.

Kade waved a finger at him. "Easy! Her name is, Ammmm...Amy? Amber?"

"And I'm sure she a very cosmopolitan, high-class...bus stop skank," Drake added.

Ajax and Sage both laughed. The joke went right past Kade.

"When did you get back?" Drake asked.

"Two days ago," Kade said. "Western Oregon. Easiest damn ride I ever did."

"Nice," Drake said. "That would explain your extra energy at Despo's last night."

Kade waved off the comment. "When did you get in?"

"Just this morning," Drake said. "I made it as far as Rock Creek late last night, stopped and camped until this morning."

"Why the hell didn't you just come on home?" Ajax said. "I was up."

"I know," Drake said. "You said you had to get the new demo done when I talked to you from Billings. Figured I'd let you work."

Ajax raised his fingertips to his brow in salute. "An unnecessary, but still noble, gesture."

Drake nodded. "You get it done?"

"Fifteen minutes before I came here."

Drake looked across at Sage. "Looks like you're the only one that got any sleep here last night Sunshine."

"Trust me, it shows," Sage replied.

"Did she just call us ugly?" Ajax asked.

"I don't know about ugly, haggard for sure," Drake said.

Before the banter could go any further, Kade raised a hand. "Fellas, don't take this the wrong way, I am glad to see you, but are we going to do any fishing this morning? If not, I have something that needs tending to."

The other three again dropped their heads over the hood of the truck and chuckled.

"Far be it for us to deny a man just returning from the wild," Drake said.

"Yeah, you go tend to whatever you need to," Ajax added.

Kade smiled, waved, and shuffled back towards his truck.

"Just be sure to make it to the bedroom this time!" Sage called back over her shoulder.

Drake and Ajax both laughed harder.

"We are all here, did you guys want to do any fishing or should we just call it a day?" Drake asked.

"Hell, I didn't even bring my rod," Ajax said.

"I have mine, but it isn't strung," Sage added.

Drake nodded. "Alright, Friday it is then."

Ajax pushed himself up from the truck and extended another fist to Drake. "See you back at the place?"

Drake returned the pound. "Be right behind you."

Ajax nodded and backpedaled towards his motorcycle. He dropped the helmet over his tangle of three inch dreadlocks and said, "See you Friday, girl."

"See ya," Sage said, pushing herself back from the truck. She turned to Drake and asked, "We still on for tonight?"

"Wouldn't miss it," Drake said.

Without another word they both loaded into their vehicles and drove away.

Above them, the first blotches of blue sky became apparent.

Behind them, Kade's truck sat in the parking lot, rocking in place.

Chapter Four

Two things tend to go hand and hand with child birth.

Bodily fluids and screaming.

As for the fluids, there was plenty. Blood, a fountain of amniotic solution, even a little urine.

All of it ran together, stained the sterile dressing surrounding the lower half of the mother. Coated the gloves and sleeves of Dr. Brice Schievers as he worked to deliver the fetus.

On the screaming side, there was none. Not from the mother during the procedure, not from the infant after delivery.

"Another one?" Bev Tiffin, head scrub nurse asked. She was in the room only to oversee her newest tech, out of sterile dress and several yards away from doctor and infant.

Dr. Schievers held the child by his feet and rotated him in the air. "Sure looks that way. Third one this year."

"Is he okay?"

The rotation of the child continued. When Dr. Schievers was done with the eyeball test, he laid him on an exam table and checked heart rate and pulse. "Okay as a newborn still riding his mother's Diazepam high can be."

Nurse Tiffin pulled a mask down from her face and shook her head. She made no effort to hide her disgust as she glanced back at the mother still lying on the table.

An OB resident was already at work stitching up her vaginal tear. There was no indication that she even knew where she was. Instead, she just stared at the wall, her eyes vacant.

"Another DZ?" Nurse Tiffin asked.

Dr. Schievers finished checking the child and handed him off to a nurse's aide to clean. "I haven't run a tox screen yet, but it looks like it. Heart rate is low, muscle response almost non-existent. No way in hell you're going to get that baby to cry."

"And the mother?"

"La-la Land," Dr. Schievers said. "She's so out of it I could amputate her leg and she wouldn't know it. Just be sitting there staring at nothing."

"Did we not know she was self-medicating when we gave her the epidural?" Nurse Tiffin asked.

"We didn't give her an epidural. She came in like that, so doped up she couldn't even tell us how much she'd taken. We couldn't risk giving her anything else, so we went right in."

Another incriminating glance towards the mother. "Jesus, was she trying to kill herself?"

"Herself? No," Dr. Schievers said. "The baby? Sure looks like it. Dr. Richards, are you good in here?"

"Yes, sir," the resident said, raising his head up just high enough to see over the mother's bent knees. "Couple more stitches and a clean-up and we're out of here."

Dr. Schievers gave a thumbs up and peeled the surgical gown and gloves from his body. He wadded them into the surgery trash can and backed away from the room, taking the chart with him.

Nurse Tiffin followed close behind. "Police or child services?"

"Both," Dr. Schievers said, pushing out into the hall. "What she tried to do was criminal. She should be behind bars, let alone near that child."

"Does she have any others?"

"I don't know, but I'll have MPD look into it."

Nurse Tiffin followed him as far as the corner of the hallway before breaking off. "What a way to start the day, right Doctor?"

"You said it," Dr. Schievers replied and waved the chart at her. His only response was a full view of the grey hair bunched in curls around her head and her squatty backside crammed into a pair of blue scrub pants.

"That's not much better," Dr. Schievers muttered and continued down the hall.

It was just seven o'clock, but already the operating ward was coming alive for the day. Fifteen minutes later and the delivery probably would have taken place in the emergency room.

That would have been bad. Very, very bad.

Two orderlies nodded hello as they pushed an obese women past him. He returned the nod and tried not to glance at her on the gurney.

Probably in for an angioplasty. Maybe a diabetes related amputation. Missoula County Hospital didn't handle liposuction or gastric bypass.

Dr. Schievers shuffled through his office door and slammed it shut behind him. He had a long day ahead of him and needed to get this done and over with.

He fished his cell-phone out of his top desk drawer and dialed the number by memory. He bypassed the chair and opted to stand, staring out at the impending dawn. The line rang only twice before a thin, nasal, female voice picked up.

"Is it done?"

"You idiots almost killed her," Dr. Schievers said. No salutation, no attempt to pretend he had anything but contempt for the people he was calling.

"*Excuse me,*" the voice shot back. The tone was sharp. The warning implicit.

Dr. Schievers pulled his focus from the world outside to his own reflection staring back at him. The day was just a couple of hours old and already dark circles lined his eyes. Each day, his thinning blonde hair retreated a little further up his scalp.

"I'm sorry," he muttered. "The girl this morning, she was in bad shape. Please tell them to dial back the Diazepam next time."

"That's what I thought you said," the female voice replied. "Is everything else in order?"

"She will be discharged later today without remembering a thing. The newborn will be turned over within a couple of days."

"And the paperwork?"

"What paperwork?"

The female snorted. "You're getting better at this whole game, Doctor. We get that temper of yours under control and this could turn out quite beneficial for all of us."

Dr. Schievers continued to stare at his own reflection in the mirror. He hated it a little more each day, but was in too far now to do anything about it. "Speaking of which..."

"The standard fee will be wired to your account when the child is collected."

"Okay, thank you," Dr. Schievers said.

The line was already dead.

He thumbed the phone closed and dropped it back into the drawer. Stood with his hands clasped behind his back. After a few moments he turned, lifted the file from the desk and fed it into his shredder.

He didn't even wait for it to complete the job before grabbing his coffee thermos and heading for the cafeteria.

It was going to be a long day.

Chapter Five

Three minutes before ten.

Drake pulled his truck to a stop in the back of the law school parking lot and hopped out. He jogged in a stiff legged shuffle as fast as his flip-flops would allow through the parking lot, sliding between cars in a direct line for the side door.

He carried nothing in his hands. He wasn't going to be here long.

The west entrance to the school was open as he stepped inside and cut a path from the rear entrance. As a third year law student he only had two classes, both of which met just once a week.

The bulk of his course load this semester was finishing up his clinical hours. The school required every student complete three hundred hours of clinical training in one of a dozen different fields before graduating.

They liked to call it job training. The students toiling through it thought of it more as indentured servitude.

Despite his light load and flexible schedule, Drake was still required to show up at the Dean's opening remarks. Thanks to the school's antiquated attendance policy, this was not the polite way of saying he wanted to go brownnose a bit.

He actually had to go, sign in, and stay the whole time.

A bit unnecessary for a place that purported itself as a professional school, but it was what it was.

His pace unwavering, Drake made it through the library and into the auditorium with a minute to spare. He scribbled his initials on the attendance forms by the door and took up his familiar spot on the back row.

The rest of the usual suspects were already there.

First on the end of the row was Mary Ann Schwartz, a single mother that seemed to go through life with an angry glare on her face. With frizzy red hair and an oversized forehead, it was possible the scowl improved her looks.

An empty seat separated her from Ben Dyke, a rancher from Eastern Montana that took the term introvert to a whole new level. In the two years Drake had known him, he'd heard Ben use a total of eleven words.

None that weren't prompted by a direct question.

Another empty seat separated Ben and the pair of corner dwellers Drake usually sat with, Greg Mooney and Wyatt Teague.

"Dammit!" Greg said. Checked his watch and motioned to Wyatt. "Another three minutes and this prick would have owed me lunch."

"Very sorry to disappoint you, sir," Drake replied, reaching out to shake his friend's hand. "And for the record, I actually made it in last night."

"Since when has that ever mattered?" Wyatt inserted. "You live a mile from campus and are late to class at least once a week."

Drake released Greg's grip and shook Wyatt's hand. "I feel like you want me to say I'm sorry right now, but I'm not."

"Hell no I don't," Wyatt said. "You just won me a free lunch."

"Very happy to be of service," Drake said, falling into a chair beside Greg.

In front of them stretched twenty even rows of chairs, broken into three sections by a pair of aisles. The front third of the room was packed tight with over-eager first years and second year students that were still jockeying for class standing.

The second third was the remainder of the second year class, all beginning to spread themselves out a bit from one another.

The rear of the room was comprised of a bored and disinterested third year class. Very few of them even attempted to hide their disdain at having to be in the auditorium.

Even less tried to pretend most of the people around them were little more than acquaintances by circumstance at this point.

"I see you're ready for another fun and exciting year here at Montana Law," Greg said, motioning to Drake's empty hands and flip-flops.

"I got three hours of sleep last night," Drake replied. "I haven't unpacked a thing from my truck, have barely seen my dog. The second this thing is over I'm out of here."

"You shitting me? What all do you have this semester?"

"Local Government on Mondays, Land Use Planning on Tuesdays. Clinic with you jokers. That's it," Drake said.

Wyatt muttered under his breath and shook his head.

Greg looked at him and said, "Classes last summer, right?"

"There it is," Drake said. "You guys thought I was crazy then, but it's making life easy now."

"Lucky bastard," Wyatt grumbled.

At the front of the room a short, diminutive man with golden hair strode to the front podium. His face was creased with a megawatt smile. He even offered a small wave as if a beauty queen riding on a float.

"Going with the blonde this year," Drake whispered.

Wyatt snorted. "Three colors in three years. That's not a bad streak."

"Impressive," Greg agreed.

"Good morning," the man said from the front of the room. "For those of you that I have not had the pleasure of meeting yet, my name is Dean Weston and it is my esteemed honor to welcome you all back here for another exciting year at Montana Law."

He paused as if waiting for applause. None came.

"I was just telling my wife this morning that this is my favorite day of the year. Better than graduation. Even better than Christmas. Does anybody here know why?"

As Weston paused again, Greg leaned over and whispered, "How long before he blinds someone in the front row with that smile?"

"Those veneers are looking quite bold today," Drake agreed.

"I myself am debating sunglasses as we speak," Wyatt intoned.

"Because of all the unknown possibilities the next nine months hold," Weston said from the podium. "Today marks the beginning of a new legal career for some of you. A final step towards entering the legal workforce for others.

"Regardless where you find yourself on your path though, today is an opportunity for you to stake your own bold claim on the legal community. To write a groundbreaking brief, challenge an unjust law, to bring a voice to the unheard masses."

"Wow, is it an election year in here or what?" Wyatt whispered.

"This year, we also have a special treat," Weston pushed on. "Due to the untimely and unfortunate destruction left by Hurricane Wanda, with us this semester are two visiting students from the Louisiana State University School of Law."

As he spoke, he motioned towards a young man marked with severe acne and a Latina with dark hair. Both half turned and nodded at the crowd. Neither looked happy to be there.

"As always, if anything should arise, my door is open," Weston said. Once more he stared out at the crowd as if waiting for a reaction.

Per usual, he looked relieved when none came.

"And with that, I wish you all well and the best of luck this year."

He still stood with his arms extended from his sides gripping the podium as most of the room rose to leave. In the back, none of the three made any effort to move.

"You boys here at all today?" Drake asked.

"Hell yes," Wyatt said. "Not all of us were smart enough to get a jump on things. Two classes this afternoon."

"Same here," Greg added.

"My condolences," Drake said. "I am heading home to eat and unpack, take Q to the park. See you back here for clinic tomorrow?"

"We'll be here," Wyatt said.

"I expect a full scouting report," Drake said, pushing himself up to go.

"Way ahead of you," Greg said. "Got most of the first years scoped and catalogued."

"That's my boy," Drake said.

"Quick heads up, Lauer stopped by before you got here," Wyatt said. "Said to wear courtroom attire tomorrow. Guess he's got a special treat for our first day."

Drake shook his head and slipped into the outgoing flow of students without another word. He nodded a few hellos, but made no effort to engage anybody in conversation.

Everybody ignored him much the same.

Chapter Six

The gravel crunched beneath Missoula County Sheriff Kirby Spore's boots as he climbed from his cruiser.

He leaned in across the front seat and grabbed his flat-brimmed hat from the passenger seat. With a practiced move, he smashed it down over the bald spot peeking through his strawberry blonde hair.

One flick of the wrist and the driver's door slammed shut, but he made no effort to move. Instead he hooked his thumbs through a belt loop on either side of his waist.

Surveyed the scene.

In front of him was a non-descript barn, brown in color. It looked almost identical to the dozens of others that dotted every field in Western Montana. Two stories, sliding front door, well maintained.

To the left was an ancient Massie-Ferguson tractor with a round bale of alfalfa stuck to the fork on the back-end. No doubt ready to be unloaded for the cows grazing in the field nearby.

Beside the tractor stood an old rancher in a pair of khaki workpants and a flannel shirt. The guy kicked at the ground, but never raised his eyes to look at anybody.

Kirby was certain he'd never seen the man before.

On the other side of the barn were two deputies. One was bent at the waist, regurgitating everything he'd eaten in the last three days into the weeds. The other was standing beside him, staring into the distance, trying not to do the same.

Spore unhooked his thumbs and walked across the driveway towards the open barn door. He could hear movement inside and as he got closer, his nose began to pick up a peculiar scent.

Not the expected smells of hay and manure and livestock. Something much more visceral.

Something a lot like charred flesh.

A pang stabbed deep into his stomach as a third deputy stepped from the barn and met him halfway across the lot. He was dressed in the same brown uniform as the two men off to the side. In addition, he had a red bandana tied across the bottom half of his face.

"Thanks for coming," the deputy said. He slid the bandana down around his neck to reveal a face that was a little pale, but holding it together.

With some grey around the temples, this wasn't his first crime scene.

Kirby waved off the comment. "What have we got?"

The deputy, a rangy man named Anson, motioned towards the rancher. "This is Bruce Meigs, owner of the P-Bar-M Ranch. Got a call from him this morning that said someone had been doing something out in his barn."

Spore waited for further explanation. It didn't come. "Someone doing something?"

Anson opened his mouth to speak. Closed it just as fast. He raised the bandana back over his face and motioned Spore to follow him inside.

Together they crossed through the sliding door into the barn. The bright sun from overhead disappeared behind them, plunging them into darkness. It took a full minute for their eyes to adjust.

It was a minute Spore barely survived. The smell of burnt skin was so strong in the air, it almost sent him running back outside.

"What the hell is that smell?" Spore muttered. He reached into his back pocket and produced a handkerchief. Pressed it to his face.

Already he could feel snot running down into his thick moustache.

"Your guess is as good as mine," Anson said. "But that's not all. Take a look at this."

He led Spore over to the center of the room and shined his flashlight down at the concrete. On the ground was enough blood to feed a family of vampires for days.

It was clear it had been there for some length of time. It was already crusted black. Sawdust and bits of hay were imbedded in it.

"Human?" Spore asked.

"No way of knowing yet," Anson said. "I have samples to take to the lab once we're done here."

"Yeah, at this point, all blood looks the same."

Anson nodded.

"Anything else?" Spore asked.

"Odd, but no," Anson said. "No further signs of a struggle. No bodies. Nothing."

"Hmm," Spore said, motioned them both outside.

Once they could breathe again, he led Anson over to his cruiser. "What have we got on this Meigs guy?"

"Very clean," Anson said. "Third generation rancher, all in the Bitterroot Valley. Ran his sheet before I came out."

"How'd he find it?"

"Comes out here once a week to feed stock. Went inside to grab his water hose, almost stepped in it."

"Any idea when this happened?"

Anson shook his head. "This is summer pasture. He only comes out once a week. Says it wasn't here last Wednesday."

"Still a pretty large window," Spore said.

"Yep."

Spore pursed his lips and wiped his hands along the front of his shirt. The sun was bright overhead, but not hot. Still, his palms were sweating.

"Listen," Spore said, "stay here and get this place processed. Before we go jumping to conclusions, make sure this wasn't a bear attack or something."

"Yes, sir."

"In the meantime, I can drop off those blood samples at the lab on my way in town."

"Sounds good," Anson said and jogged off to his own cruiser.

A moment later he returned with a handheld cooler and extended it to Spore.

Spore nodded to him and tossed the cooler and his hat both onto the passenger seat. With his chin he motioned towards the two deputies still bent over by the side of the barn. "And get those damn newbies out of here. It's embarrassing."

Anson smirked. "Aye aye, Sheriff."

Spore did a three point turn and maneuvered his cruiser back towards Missoula. He waited until the barn disappeared in his rearview, then flipped open his cell-phone.

A thin, nasal, female voice answered on the first ring. "Yes?"

"There might be a problem."

"We don't deal with *might* here Sheriff. You know that. Is there, or isn't there?"

"There is not," Spore said, sighing. "But I am calling as a courtesy to request people clean up there messes in the future."

The woman didn't ask for further elaboration. "It was a one time thing."

"I know," Spore said. “I was there.”

"Is it under control?"

"Yes."

The word was just out before the line went dead.

"Bitch," Spore muttered. He swung the cruiser in behind an Exxon station and pulled to a stop alongside the dumpster out back. In three short steps he hopped out and emptied the contents of the cooler into it.

He was back on the road less than thirty seconds later.

Chapter Seven

You're late.

Drake got the text message and smirked. Typed out a response.

Picnic tables.

A moment later the double doors leading from the rear of the Saint Michael's cafeteria burst open and Sage emerged.

"How long have you been out here?"

"Just a few minutes," Drake said. He was perched atop one of the tables with his bare feet resting on the bench seat. Beside him was an unmarked pizza box. "Didn't want dinner to get cold."

Sage walked across the grassy expanse between them and bypassed the pizza. Instead she went to Drake and wrapped her arms around his neck.

"Hey there," Drake said, returning the hug. "So a trip to the Firetower is what it takes to get some love around here these days?"

Sage released the hug and punched his shoulder. "I always show you love. I just didn't get a chance to this morning."

"I see," Drake said. "Hungry?"

The dinners had started about a year before, every Wednesday night.

When Sage was first hired on at St. Michael's she had drawn the second shift. Far and away the least desired timeslot in the building. Half a day spent with bosses looking over your shoulder. The other half spent inside while everyone else is enjoying their evening.

Most people endured twelve months on the second shift. Sage was now approaching two full years. Some speculated it was so she would be available to run with the Zoo Crew every morning, though she had never admitted it.

To help ease the pain of never seeing a free evening, Drake started meeting her for dinner every Wednesday. Sometimes he brought food. Sometimes they bought whatever the cafeteria was serving.

Always, they talked and laughed a lot.

"I'm always hungry for pizza," Sage said, peeling back the lid and grabbing a slice. "Why are we outside? Missing the Montana evenings?"

"Not as much as I was missing the Firetower," Drake said, following her into the pizza box. "And my girl."

Sage gave him a quizzical look.

Drake responded by pursing his lips and making a two-note whistle. On cue, a bulldog emerged from the bushes across the courtyard. Short and squat, she was red brindle in color with a splash of white down her face and front paws.

Sage laughed. "You brought Suzy Q with you to the hospital. Of course you did."

"Of course I did," Drake echoed. "Besides, there was no way this girl was going to let me out of her sight. I may have to take her to court with me tomorrow."

Sage chuckled again. "I bet. Old girl missed her man. I still don't know why you didn't just take her back with you."

Drake tore off a chunk of crust and tossed it to the dog. "She never would have survived the Nashville heat. It was triple digits most of the summer."

"You have air conditioning," Sage replied.

Drake exhaled and finished his slice. "It wouldn't have been fair to her. I was working a ton. Finishing up stuff at the house the rest of the time."

Sage nodded. "How is all that coming along?"

"It's done," Drake said. He offered no further explanation. Reached for more pizza instead.

In front of them, Suzy Q sniffed the ground in a circle. Her loud breathing and snorting filled the empty air space.

"And around here?" Drake asked. "Wild and crazy summer?"

Sage made a face at his blatant change of subject, but let it pass. "Eh. Ajax and I hit the water a time or two, but it isn't the same without you and Kade around."

Drake eyed her. "Not quite what I was referring to."

Starting on her second slice as well, Sage shrugged. "You didn't hear? That crashed and burned. No survivors. Search called off."

"Ouch," Drake said, wincing. "My condolences."

"Oh yes, very tragic."

"Last week when we talked you said it was rocky. I didn't realize that meant combustible."

"Got worse as the summer went on. I think the idea of you all returning, and my constant talking about it, had him wound pretty tight. Started trying to suggest I bow out of the Crew."

Drake stopped eating for a moment and turned to face her. "You're kidding me."

"Like I said, fiery crash," Sage said, finishing off her pizza.

"Understandably so," Drake said. "Sorry to hear that."

"It happens," Sage deadpanned. "Happened to you just last winter."

"That it did."

Sage slid her gaze up from Suzy Q to Drake. "I should be getting back inside."

"Already?" Drake asked. "Feels like we just sat down. We've got a lot more ground to cover."

"Time flies," Sage said, smiling as she bent to scratch behind Suzy Q's ears.

"You want the rest of this pie? I'm sure there's some staff in there that will take it off your hands."

Sage rose to full height. "Just like I'm sure there's a gamer at home that would take it off yours."

"Already have one in the truck for him," Drake said. "I mean, he did watch my dog this summer."

"Well, in that case," Sage said, accepting the box as Drake stood and gave her another hug.

"See you Friday?"

"I'll be there," Sage replied.

"I'll be there first," Drake said with a smile. He whistled once more and smacked the side of his leg.

The sun dropped a little lower over the horizon as the two sides went in opposite directions.

Sage and the pizza back inside. Drake and Suzy Q back towards the parking lot.

Chapter Eight

Of all the shit Drake put up with over the summer, wearing a tie was the worst part.

The entire thing felt like an exercise in tedium. Seventy-five of the eighty hours he worked each week were spent inside a windowless office. There were four other employees total. Three middle-aged men and one older woman.

He wasn't trying to impress any of them with his appearance. They damned sure weren't trying to impress him.

The other five hours a week he spent talking to his clients. On Death Row. He would have had a better chance of fitting in with a biker vest and two full sleeves of ink.

Again, tedium.

Thursday morning Drake returned from his run to the unhappy reminder that on his first real day back, he had to put the monkey suit back on. He stalled as long as he could.

Watched Ajax demonstrate the new project he was working on. Took Q for a walk. Watched the clock tick on towards nine before relenting and getting dressed.

Solid charcoal Brooks Brothers suit. Black pinstriped dress shirt. Patterned tie.

It was all a little rumpled from the trip out, but he didn't care. Besides, in Montana, even with the wrinkles he would be the best dressed guy in the room.

The parking lot was a little less full than it had been the day before. Without the mandatory pre-game speech from Weston hanging over their head, most students stayed far away until the absolute last second they had to report.

Drake knew the feeling.

He pulled his shoulder bag with laptop and legal pad from the front seat and made his way to the clinic room. Tucked away in the basement of the newly renovated law school, it had been upgraded from the size of a closet to a mud room.

Five desks were spread around the space. Two on either side for students. One on the back wall for Professor Lauer.

Not that there was any chance of five people ever working being seated at the same time. No way they would all fit.

Greg and Wyatt were both already there when Drake arrived. They had chosen the two desks on the right side of the room and were reclined in their chairs talking.

Drake's earlier assessment proved to be true. Greg was dressed in a pair of faded slacks, short sleeve shirt and tie loosened at the collar. Wyatt in a polo and khakis.

Montana courtroom attire.

Wyatt made a show of checking his bare wrist as Drake dropped his bag down on the opposite desk. "Well now, with seven minutes to spare. You're getting better."

Drake peeled his suit coat off and laid it atop his bag. "Remind me how it is you guys are early? Do you *like* being here all the time?"

Greg shrugged. "There are worse places to be."

"Like where?" Drake asked, dropping down into a chair and stretching his legs out in front of him.

The two exchanged a look. "And here we thought a summer spent in the coal mines of legal defense might have brought you around on being a lawyer."

"I was a little bit south of the coal mines, if you get my drift," Drake deadpanned.

They didn't get his drift.

"Hell," Drake finished for them. "I was in hell. I even preferred going to Death Row and meeting with my clients over sitting in that damn cubicle writing briefs."

Wyatt chuckled. Greg gave a look of faux sadness. "Does that mean you don't have tons of stories for us about late nights and southern women?"

"Had plenty of late nights and southern barbecue, but not women," Drake said. "Besides, weren't you supposed to have the ladies scouted out for me this morning?"

Greg extended a finger into the air. "Yes!" He spun around and took up a sheaf of wrinkled papers from his desk. "Alright, here we go. I'm skipping over our class for obvious reasons."

"They've already shot you down," Wyatt said.

"Many times," Drake added.

"Moving on to the second year class," Greg said, his voice slightly louder. "Sadly, we saw one very eligible lady obtain a left hand ring this summer and another take a walk down the aisle. In total, that leaves us with just Sarah Werner, Callie Nystrom, and a whole lot of nothing."

"I hope you have daughters one day," Drake inserted.

"And for the part you've all been waiting on, the fresh meat. This year's 1L class skews young, with very few have rings. Also, many are from out-of-state, meaning the odds of long term attachments are minimal."

"So what you're trying to say is?" Wyatt prompted.

"There will be no better time to strike," Greg said with complete authority. "No less than eight viable options. Low hanging fruit, there for the taking."

He and Wyatt both exchanged an enthusiastic high-five.

Drake sat and shook his head at them. Neither one stood taller than five-seven. Greg had bright red hair and a paunch while Wyatt had severely thinning brown hair and knock-knees.

How either one thought the first-years were low hanging fruit was beyond him.

How he had become friends with the two of them, at times, was an even greater mystery.

"But wait, he's not done yet," Wyatt said.

"There's more?" Drake asked. "New professor?"

"Even better," Greg said. "Transfer student."

"The two Weston introduced yesterday?"

"If by two you mean beauty and the beast, yes," Wyatt said.

"I don't have all the details yet, not even her name, but I will soon," Greg said.

Drake said nothing. Instead he cocked a half smile and rubbed his forehead. It was just a few minutes past nine, but already it was starting to hurt.

At least this was all that stood between him and the weekend.

"Ava Zargoza," a voice said from the door.

The unexpected sound snapped Drake's head up. He turned to see a young woman standing with her hand on her hip, a cloth sack in her hand.

"And I am *not* a transfer student," Ava said. "I was forced here. There's no way I would have chosen to come to this shithole."

Greg and Wyatt both remained motionless. Their mouths sat agape. Across from them, Drake studied the newest arrival.

She was dressed in a navy blue sheath dress with a matching business jacket. Peep-toe shoes. A string of pearls around her neck.

At least he no longer felt overdressed.

Disdain rolled off of her in waves. Drake was unsure how much she had heard, but any of it would be enough to explain the hostility.

"And let me help you out on those details," she continued. She focused her dark eyes on Greg. "None of you have a chance in hell with me. End of story."

The color drained from Greg and Wyatt's faces in unison.

Drake thought for a second they both might cry.

Luckily, Professor Lauer showed up in time to end the icy encounter before any serious blood was drawn.

"I see we're all here and ready," he said, sliding past Ava and into the room. He walked straight across to the desk reserved for him on the back wall. Picked up a thin file and tucked it under his arm. "I trust everyone here knows each other?"

Greg and Wyatt both remained frozen, mortified looks on their faces. Ava studied her toes.

"We've met," Drake said.

"Excellent!" Professor Lauer said. "As much as I would love to provide a little bit of background this morning, the hearing starts in twenty-five minutes. Shall we?"

He held a tweed clad arm towards the door. Motioned for everyone to step outside.

If he noticed the icy tension in the room, he didn't show it in the least.

Chapter Nine

Themis.

Otherwise known as Lady Justice.

Descended down from Hellenic mythology, always seen holding the Scales of Justice. On one side truth, the other fairness. In most depictions she is seen wearing a blindfold to symbolize objectivity.

However the scales balance is how the verdict is read.

Rather noble, in a philosophical sort of way.

Hokey as hell when painted on the wall of a Judge's chambers.

Either way, the painting was the first thing requested by the Honorable Minot Tanner when he took office thirteen years before. From then on, Lady Justice, in all her robed glory, oversaw every case he handled.

The room was completely packed, as adoption cases often were. Most of the time the items that come across the docket were for theft, vandalism, driving under the influence. Property line disputes, nuisance cases, public disturbances.

It is rare that a court has cause for celebration. When it does, the people turn out in droves to be a part of the festivities.

The chambers were arranged in a simple design. Bookcases lined either side wall. The rear was covered with *Themis*. The front housed the main entry with long wooden benches on either side.

In the middle of the room was an oversized desk of polished cherry. The bare wood gleamed under the fluorescent lights. Everything had been spit-shined for the occasion.

Behind the desk sat Judge Tanner himself, a large man with silver hair parted to the side and oiled in place.

On the other side of the desk was a row of chairs holding the guests of honor. Starting at the right were the new adoptive parents, Hank and Janet Wright. In Janet's arms was an infant boy not more than four or five months in age.

Beside them sat Missoula County Chief of Children's Services Patricia Harken. To her left was the attorney handling the case for the family, Riley Bennett.

Scads of fold-out chairs had been set up behind them, every one filled with eager family and friends. Many of the dabbed at the corners of their eyes. Many of the men fidgeted in place.

All of them smiled.

Making up the rear of the room were the two benches. On one side was a handful of court employees. On the other, a handful of law students and their professor as special guests to witness the proceedings.

"Unlike most of the hearings I preside over," Judge Tanner began, "this one is far less formal. Not only are we tucked away here in my chambers to maintain confidentiality, but the actual business portion of the morning will take just a few minutes. After that you are all invited to stay and take as many pictures with myself, with each other, with Lady Justice behind me as you'd like."

The room all leaned forward and nodded.

"Okay," he continued. "Today I call this special hearing in order to confirm the adoption of infant Caleb to prospective parents Hank and Janet Wright."

He turned to Harken. "Ms. Harken, as Chief of Children's Services for the County of Missoula, have the Wright's completed all necessary paperwork for this proceeding here today?"

Harken, dressed in a light grey skirt suit with pink undershirt nodded. "They have Your Honor."

"And they have completed the full application process? Including a thorough background check and active site assessment by your office?"

"They have."

"And it is the belief of your office that they are fit and able parents? And that taking custody of young Caleb will be in the best interests of the child?"

"Without reservation, it is."

"Thank you," Judge Tanner said. "Mr. Bennett, you are the supervising attorney for the Wright's, are you not?"

"I am, Your Honor," Bennett replied. Out of habit he started to rise when speaking. Caught himself and dropped back into his chair.

"And the Wright's have met all legal pre-requisites to becoming the adoptive parents of Caleb?"

"They have, Your Honor." Bennett's face and skin appeared to be nudging fifty, though his hair was still as black as the Armani suit he wore.

"Very well," Judge Tanner said. "And Mr. and Mrs. Wright, you have been made aware by Ms. Harken, Mr. Bennett, of all requirements that come with adopting a child? Legal, moral, parental?"

Both parents murmured in the affirmative.

"And it is still your desire to become the legally adoptive parents of this child?"

Both smiled and nodded with vigor.

"Very well," Judge Tanner said, "then it is with great pride and much joy that I declare you to be the new legal guardians of Caleb Wright. May the court wish you and your entire family the best of luck moving forward."

He stood and reached across the desk to shake the new parent's hands. He then worked his way across, getting Bennett and Harken as well.

Behind them, the extended Wright family stood and bunched around Hank and Janet. Women cried. Men slapped each other on the back.

After the initial euphoria of the moment, the scene settled into a marathon of picture taking. The Judge and the infant. The new parents and the infant. The Judge, the new parents and the infant.

For his part, Judge Tanner smiled and let the family take as many pictures as they wished. When they were done with him, he stepped to the side and allowed the family to use his desk and the mural behind it.

He waved goodbye to his friend Professor Jon Lauer from the law school as he and his students departed. Nodded to the other staff members as they trickled back to their offices.

After a full half-hour, the family, thanking him profusely, drifted off to continue their celebration elsewhere.

What remained was just him, Harken, and Bennett.

"Should we make the call now, or would you like me to do it later?" Judge Tanner asked.

"Go ahead. Put it on speakerphone," Bennett replied. "They want to hear from all of us anyway."

Judge Tanner shrugged and pulled his cell-phone from the desk. This was a call he never made from his office line.

Par for the course, it took only two rings for the line to be snatched up. "How did it go?"

Same thin, nasal, female voice they always heard. None of them cared if they ever heard it again. They just knew when they did, things got done.

Or else.

"Went off without a hitch," Judge Tanner said.

"Are Harken and Bennett there with you?"

"Yes," Harken replied.

"Right here," Bennett added.

"Any problems on your ends?"

"None," Harken said.

"Not a one," Bennett said.

The line went dead. Judge Tanner looked at his cohorts and shrugged. Closed the phone.

"All things considered, that wasn't so bad," he said.

"I've had worse," Bennett said.

"We all have," Harken agreed.

Judge Tanner nodded. "Any idea when the next one might occur?"

"There was a new delivery yesterday," Harken said. "My office will be taking custody tomorrow. Give it a few months and we'll be ready."

"Word is another is due a few weeks from now," Bennett said. "They need to slow these down or were going to have to start going elsewhere. How many adoptions can a town like Missoula have in a given year?"

Judge Tanner nodded in agreement. "Is there a buyer lined up for the new one yet?"

"Oh yes," Bennett said. "And they were rushed to the top of the list. Deep pockets. Just missed out on little Caleb here this morning."

Judge Tanner shook his head. Every bit of goodwill the hearing had generated within him was already gone.

A sour taste filled his mouth.

"Alright everyone, I guess that's it for us here today. Keep me posted about when the next one is scheduled or if there is anything else I can do to help."

Harken and Bennett both nodded their assent and disappeared without another word.

Chapter Ten

Coffee.

The front end to a pair of beverages that most lawyers never go a day without consuming. The second one takes various forms, but always serves as the polar opposite.

One brings them up. The other pulls them down.

Professor Lauer led his clinic group from the judge's chambers and down to the lower level of the courthouse. At the far end, tucked just inside the exit door, was a small lunch counter serving sandwiches, sodas, and the almighty brown energy source of attorneys the world over.

"Can I get you guys anything?" he asked, ordered a large black.

Greg opted for a medium cappuccino. Wyatt went with a latte.

In all the time Drake had known them, he never knew either one to turn down anything free.

Ava declined anything. He did the same.

Drinks in hand, Professor Lauer wove out from the bowels of the courthouse to the front lawn. He took the four of them to a picnic table under a towering oak tree. Waited as they settled in around it.

Overhead the sun was a golden hue, beating down on them. The temperature hovered at an even sixty-five degrees. A slight breeze blew through town, pushing west out of the Hellgate Canyon.

Despite the weather, the air around the table was still frosty. Ava was pissed. Greg and Wyatt were both petrified.

Drake was indifferent.

"Alright," Lauer said, standing at the end of the table, cup in hand. He was a small man, with a very thin thatch of sandy brown hair combed to the side. He stood just a few inches above five feet tall. "Very sorry for the rush this morning, but I had some things to get done before the hearing.

"Speaking of which, the reason I dragged you all over here today was three-fold. First, to start you off with a few free clinic hours. You might not think you'll need them, and the odds are you won't, but it's better to have too many than not enough.

"Second, I wanted to give you a little taste of the courthouse. I'm not sure if you guys have been down here before, so I wanted to get your feet wet without actually having to do anything.

"Third, and most important, I wanted to start the semester off on a high point. After practicing law for over twenty years, I can attest that there are times when this job is nothing short of soul crushing. That's why when you have a chance to get a win, to see something positive like the hearing this morning, you take it."

Across the table, Greg and Wyatt both sipped their drinks. Everyone remained silent.

Lauer took a long pull on his own coffee and said, "Alright, with that, I guess, welcome to clinic. As you all know, we are the Missoula Legal Services division. We provide representation to the poor and indigent people of Missoula free of charge.

"The office is located downtown on Pinckney Street and you will all be required to maintain office hours at some point each week. To be honest though, the place is a dump and if I were you I would work in the clinic office at the Law School as much as possible.

"Most of what you'll see pass through will be basic stuff. Landlord disagreements. Welfare disputes. Maybe a minor in possession.

"Nothing too strenuous.

"My role here is more of a mentor, not necessarily a guide. When something comes in, use each other, use the school resources.

If questions linger, then come to me. The whole idea of the program is to provide practical application to all the theory you've been learning the last two years.

"If you want a babysitter, there are plenty of other clinics that specialize in hand holding. No hard feelings."

He paused and waited for any response. The statement was not made in anger. Was not issued as a challenge. As an adjunct professor, Lauer had a very full plate. This was just how he operated.

It was the reason Drake, Greg, and Wyatt had signed up with him in the first place.

"Alright then," Lauer said. "Consider our first clinic meeting adjourned. I have to run back inside to speak to a few people, but you guys work out an office hours schedule starting on Monday. I'll see you all soon."

He raised his cup in a farewell salute and disappeared back inside. The second he was gone, Ava rose and walked off.

She didn't even look at the rest of the table, let alone speak to them.

Greg and Wyatt still looked petrified as the remaining three stood to leave. Nobody said anything as they circled the building back to Wyatt's car.

"How much do you think she heard this morning?" Greg asked.

"I'd say she pretty well already answered that," Drake replied.

"Do you really think none of us have a chance with her?" Wyatt asked.

Drake looked at the duo and snorted. Said nothing.

The three walked on in silence. They moved on to the main walkway past a row of metal benches.

As they did, a blonde girl a couple of years younger stood fidgeting in front of them. She bit her bottom lip several times before asking, "Is one of you Drake Bell?"

Her voice no more than a whisper.

The mortification melted fell away from Greg and Wyatt. They exchanged sly glances and Greg tossed his head to Drake. "Right there's the man you're looking for."

The girl gave a timid smile. "Hi."

Drake narrowed his eyes. Twisted his head a bit to the side. "Hi?"

"Can we talk?"

Wyatt reached out and rapped Drake on the arm. "We've got class at eleven, so we're going to head back. See you over there later?"

Campus was over a dozen blocks away and Drake was wearing in a suit. The last thing he wanted to do was walk back to get his truck.

At the same time, he didn't seem to have another option. "Sure."

He waited for Greg and Wyatt to depart and asked, "I'm very sorry, but do I know you?"

The girl glanced quickly around. "Do you mind if we walk and talk?"

The question took Drake by surprise. "Uh, okay?"

In silence, they started down the main path. They walked out to Broadway Avenue, cut across a few side streets, came out along the banks of the Clark Fork River.

This time of year, the spring run-off was long gone. The river moved in an easy flow, cutting the town in half from east to west.

Drake shrugged off his suit jacket and folded it over his shoulder bag. Rolled his sleeves up to the forearm.

"So, not to be rude," he began.

"No," the girl said, cutting him off. "You don't know me. And after today, the odds are you'll see me rarely, if ever, again."

"I see," Drake said. The situation was growing stranger by the minute. Still, he kept a bevy of questions locked away. "So why are we talking now then?"

"My name is Ella Haggerty. I believe you know my cousin Beth?"

Drake was good with faces. Better with names. Instantly he placed it in an instant.

Senior year, biology class.

"Yeah, she and I went to school together. She saved my hide when I missed a few classes with a concussion. How's she doing?"

Ella shook her head. "She asked me to come find you."

Drake started to say something, but stopped short. It had taken a moment for the words to register. "Wait, *find* me? She has my email. Why didn't she just drop me a line?"

"That's not what I meant," Ella said.

Drake paused. "She didn't ask you to find her friend Drake. She asked you to find the third year law student Drake."

Ella nodded. "Yeah. I went to the law school this morning and asked around. They said you were in court. You'd be the tall one in a suit."

"Still, why didn't she do it? Is she okay?" Drake asked.

Ella kept her head turned towards the water. Below, a pair of kayakers floated by. On the opposite bank a man lobbed tennis balls into the water for his golden retriever to fetch.

"No," Ella whispered. She didn't look at Drake, but he could tell her eyes were glassy.

"What's going on?"

Ella shook her head. "It's not my story to tell. She just told me to track you down and ask if you would meet with her."

Drake exhaled. "And you can't tell me any more than that? Just that she's not okay and would like to meet?"

A pair of bicyclers passed them on the right. After that came a jogger pushing a baby stroller along the asphalt river walk path.

"I'm sorry," Ella said. "I can't say more because if you decide not to meet with her..."

She let her voice trail off.

"What?" Drake asked. "What happens if I don't meet with her?"

"I don't know," Ella whispered. A crack was obvious in her voice.

They came to the Madison Street Bridge and Ella stopped. She turned and faced Drake, sniffled. "Listen, I understand how this looks and sounds. I do. But she wouldn't be asking and I wouldn't be here unless it was important."

Drake's mouth dropped open. He said nothing.

"Are you familiar with the website GoGriz.com?"

Drake made a confused face. "Yeah?"

"There's a fan discussion page on there with a thread entitled 'Too early for Cat/Griz tickets?' All you have to do is respond yes or no."

The information settled in on Drake. "And if I say yes?"

"Instructions for how to meet will be posted to look like a ticket exchange."

"And if I say no?"

Ella again shook her head. "I honestly don't know."

Drake nodded. Grunted. "Again, why all the clandestine measures? Doesn't she have a phone?"

"If you meet with her, she'll explain everything. If you don't, it's better you know as little as possible," Ella said.

In one quick step she moved to Drake's side, rose to her toes, kissed him on the cheek. Just as fast she was gone, striding back towards downtown.

Drake watched her go for a moment. Shook his head and crossed the bridge towards campus.

Chapter Eleven

Caddis fly.

No more than a quarter inch in length, they spend their first several months living in or adjacent to water.

Once full grown, they look like tiny moths. Wings tented on their backs. Hair-like antennae extended out in front of them.

Most people have never even heard of a caddis fly.

To a fly-fisherman, they are a Godsend.

Trout, of all forms, gobble caddis flies up starting at the first hatch in June. Keep eating them clear through the first frost in late September.

This particular morning, the caddis flies were being quite good to the Zoo Crew. Spaced out along McCully Flats two miles south of the Clark Fork, they had been in place since before dawn.

For the first actual day back, it had been an very productive morning.

Standing up to his knees in the river, Drake counted off an overhand cast and dropped his line out into the current in front of him. The moving water caught his fly and pushed it downstream, settling it atop an eddy.

Just visible atop the water, Drake focused in and waited. There was a brown trout lying along the bottom and he knew it. It was only a matter of getting its attention.

The caddis fly didn't disappoint.

With a thunderous smack, the brownie rose up from the riverbed and snatched it off the top of the water. The second Drake saw the swirl he jerked back on his rod to set the hook.

For a moment he felt the familiar tug of the fish as it fought to free itself from the metal intrusion.

Then, just like that, it was gone.

Nothing remained but the loose feeling of an empty line as Drake reeled it back in.

"Whoa!" Ajax taunted from a hundred yards downriver. "There's something you don't see every day!"

Standing out at point, everybody in the group had seen the miss. Behind him, he could hear Kade and Sage laughing as well.

Drake raised his hand in a wave to acknowledge them. Didn't turn around. Didn't want them to see the embarrassed smile on his face.

Ajax was right, it *was* something that didn't happen every day.

Drake reeled his line all the way in and hooked his fly into the third eyelet of his rod. Pulled the string tight and waded back up on to the bank.

It had been a good morning on the water.

Hell, *all* mornings were good mornings on the water.

Still, he was distracted. His mind wasn't in it.

"Oh, so you miss one and you're done for the day?" Sage called. "Just going to take your ball and go home?"

Drake smiled, waved again. Said nothing.

He leaned his rod against a downed log on the gravel bank and unsnapped the shoulder straps on his waders. Dropped the rubber leggings to the ground and walked out of them, revealing a pair of gym shorts and t-shirt underneath.

Stepping into a pair of running shoes he'd left on the bank, he spread his waders out to dry. Lowered himself to the ground and leaned back against the log.

In front of him, Kade finished the roll cast he was working and hooked his line to the pole. He splashed his way up onto the bank and started to remove his waders as well.

"Where you at today, huh?"

Drake didn't take his eyes from the water moving before him. From the sunlight dancing on the water and the polished stones beneath. "Right here."

"Uh-uh," Kade said. "I've never seen you miss a fish like that. Damn sure never seen you stop after a mistake."

Drake exhaled slowly. Shook his head. "Distracted this morning."

Kade tossed his waders out beside Drake's. "Distracted? On the first morning back?"

"Yeah," Drake said. "There's this girl."

Kade settled on the log. "That's my boy. Bout damn time."

"That's not what I meant."

"Hey, no judgment here," Kade said. He even waved a hand for emphasis. "I've been after you for years to sample the local fare."

"No offense sir, but there isn't much fare left after you get done."

"Touché," Kade conceded.

The sound of crunching gravel pulled both their heads to the right. Sage was walking towards them, pole in one hand, fly box in the other.

"You boys done?" she asked.

Kade ignored the question. "Drake met a girl!"

"Oh?" Sage asked. Made a face. "And that's relevant to quitting early how?"

"You see him miss that fish? She's in his head already," Kade said.

Drake turned back to the water. Shook his head again. "That's not what I said. It's not like that."

Sage unhooked her waders. "So what's it like?"

"She came to see me yesterday," Drake said. He looked at Kade. Pushed on before his friend could interject again. "Not me the person, me the law student."

"Damn," Kade said.

"You don't know the half of it," Drake said.

"So tell us," Sage prompted. She laid her waders out beside the others. Took up a spot on the log opposite Kade.

Drake exhaled. Debated the question. "I trust this goes no further than the Crew?"

Neither said anything. They didn't have to.

"Senior year there was a girl in one of my classes. Nice girl. Very quiet. I barely even knew her, but when I got my concussion and missed a few weeks she went out of her way to help me. After that, we remained friends but sort of drifted apart.

"Haven't seen her in over a year. To be honest, haven't even thought about her in over six months."

In quick fashion, he relayed the story to them about the encounter with Ella the day before. As he did so, Ajax joined them. Sprawled out flat on the gravel and listened.

When he was done, nobody said anything for several minutes. They all chewed the info in their own way.

"So that's why you were so quiet last night," Ajax said. Statement, not a question.

"Was I?" Drake asked.

"You took Q for three walks. She's a damned bulldog. A trip to the mailbox could last her a week."

Drake smirked. He hadn't thought about it, but Ajax was right. This had been gnawing on him for the better part of a day now.

"What do you think is wrong?" Sage asked.

"I have no idea," Drake said. "I keep wracking my brain on it too. What could be bad enough to send a cousin to set up some kind of cloak-and-dagger meeting? But not bad enough to just call the police?"

"You guys ever hook up?" Kade asked. "Maybe you're a daddy and didn't know it? She's got the herps and thinks you should get tested?"

Drake turned his head. Glared through the one eye facing Kade. Said nothing.

"Alright," Kade said, holding his hands up. "Just asking."

"Not all of us wake up every day in fear that our next case of rug burn could be our last," Ajax said.

He didn't aim it at Kade, but he didn't have to. The implication was clear.

In the first days of the Crew, Sage would scold the guys for such suggestive talk. Now, she let it pass without comment.

"So what are you going to do?" Kade asked, steering the conversation into safer waters.

"He's going to go," Sage said.

"He is?" Ajax asked.

"I am?" Drake responded.

Sage leaned forward, rested her elbows on her knees. "Of course you are. You wouldn't be you otherwise."

"A guy with a hero complex?" Drake asked.

"I didn't say that. But you're a good guy. If someone is in trouble and you can help, you'll try to."

"Hmm," Drake said.

"I mean, that is why you went to law school, right?" she added.

Drake turned his gaze back to the water. Watched the sun appear over the aspen trees to his right. Drew in the cool Montana morning air.

Said nothing.

Chapter Twelve

Sage was right.

The minute Drake got home, he signed onto GoGriz.com and responded.

Yes, but I have a pair of tickets I need to get rid of. $50 each. Meet to discuss?

From there he showered, ate, walked Suzy Q around the yard. By the time he headed towards the law school, the sun was high above. The sleepy mountain town was awake and functional.

Not Monday through Thursday functional, but close.

Dressed in a pair of khaki shorts, v-neck and sandals, he avoided the bulk of the school and took the back stairwell down to the clinic office. He could hear a great deal of commotion out in the halls and had no interest in being a part of it.

Regardless what Greg's scouting report said, he would stay far away from first years for as long as he could.

The clinic office was empty as he stepped inside and settled into the same desk he used the day before. Across the room he could see Greg and Wyatt had already put some things onto their respective spaces as well.

Neither was around. After yesterday, they weren't going anywhere near Ava for a while.

For her part, the fourth desk was bare.

Drake set up his laptop and fished through his shoulder bag. Pulled out a legal pad and a stack of reading for Local Government on Monday. He still hadn't convinced himself that he was back to the grind yet, but he would go through the motions for at least a little while anyway.

Internally, he set the over/under at an hour.

He didn't even make it that far.

After his third consecutive article discussing the city government decision making hierarchy, he pushed the reading aside. Brought his laptop to life. Made the usual passes through his gmail and yahoo accounts. Took a quick pass through facebook.

Went to the site he'd been avoiding since he got there. GoGriz.com.

Why he was avoiding it, he didn't know. Maybe it was because he didn't want to stare at a message posting that had no chance of being answered yet. Maybe it was because he wasn't sure if he wanted it to be answered at all.

Either way, he didn't have to wonder long. There were two messages waiting for him.

That's great. When can you meet?

The tickets are a gift. Can we meet this morning? I was hoping to surprise a friend with them.

Drake leaned back in his chair. Made a face. He had not expected to hear a word from her at ten-thirty on a Friday morning. Definitely not two pleas to meet ASAP.

Sure. I'm on campus now. The tickets are with me. When/Where?

This time he left the browser to the discussion forum open. He didn't know why, but he had a feeling a response was imminent.

He was right.

Food Zoo. 11.

Drake exhaled once more. That was less than twenty minutes away. Beth was close, and she was in a hurry.

Which may mean desperate.

I'll meet you by the front entrance. Thanks!

Drake closed the browser and pushed it away from himself. Reached out and shut his laptop. An uneasy feeling sat in his stomach.

This morning he had been certain he was doing the right thing. The only thing. Now, he wasn't quite so sure.

He glanced up at the clock on the wall and tried for a moment to return to reading. Made it less than a paragraph before shuffling the papers into a pile and stuffing them back in his bag.

The reading would have to wait.

"I didn't think anybody would be here this morning," a voice said behind him. The sound was unexpected, shattering the silence of the room.

Drake jerked towards it with a start. His heart rate picked up a bit.

In front of him stood Ava.

She was dressed down from her courtroom ensemble of a day before. Still way overdressed for most any event in the state of Montana, let alone law school.

Black skirt, pumps, white blouse. Same pearls.

"On my way out in just a minute," Drake said.

Ava carried a load of books and supplies in her arms. Walked past him and dropped them with a thud on her desk. "I take it this is my spot?"

"I do believe so." Drake rose, half bent at the waist, and extended a hand to her. "Drake Bell."

Ava stared at the hand, then him. Accepted the shake. "Ava Zargoza."

Drake smirked. "Uh, yeah. I caught that yesterday."

Ava pursed her lips a bit. "Yeah, sorry about that. This whole situation just..."

Drake decided to switch topics. "When did you get here?"

"Three days ago," Ava said.

Neither of their tones were hostile, but they weren't friendly either. More like a deadpan conversation between business associates.

"Yeah, Missoula takes some getting used to," Drake said. He considered adding more, thought better of it.

"I hope I'm not here long enough to find out," Ava said.

Drake made a face. "If you don't mind my asking, why'd you pick UM?"

Ava sighed and stared at the wall in front of her. "I didn't. After the hurricane hit, a bunch of schools contacted LSU about accepting last second transfers until the place reopened.

"Of course, being LSU, the dumbasses didn't let us choose by class rank. Instead they used alphabetical order."

Drake nodded. "And you being Zargoza?"

"Yep. The other guy chose this hellhole. I got stuck here."

Drake debated continuing the conversation. Decided against it. There hadn't been any overt hostility between them. That was good enough for their first actual encounter.

He left without another word.

Chapter Thirteen

Even for the third day of class, the Food Zoo was a madhouse.

Built in the late eighties as a part of campus expansion, it housed a burrito bar, a pizza counter, an off-brand sandwich joint. Down the hall was a coffee shop. Around the corner was a dining hall.

Unless someone wanted to go off-campus or pack lunch every day, the Food Zoo was pretty much the only game in town.

Drake cut a diagonal through the grassy quad in the middle of campus, past the undergrads playing Frisbee. Past the hippies trying to balance themselves on a rope strung between two trees.

He arrived at the front entrance two minutes before eleven to find Beth already there and waiting on him. If she hadn't spotted him and waved as he approached, he might have walked right on by her.

Her white blonde hair, ruddy cheeks and watery blue eyes were the same as always. As he approached though, he didn't notice any of that.

All he saw was a girl in her third trimester of pregnancy.

"Oh, it's so good to see you," she said as he approached. Rocked up onto her toes and wrapped one arm around his neck.

"Uh, you too," Drake said, patting her back with one hand. Her prodigious bulge bumped against his hip, making the entire situation very awkward.

"Just go with it," Beth whispered into his ear. "They might be watching."

"Who?" Blake whispered back, but Beth had already released the hug.

"Shall we?" she asked, waving a hand inside.

"Uh, sure?" Drake said. He was doing his best to play along, despite his confusion.

Together they slid into the current of people going inside and let it carry them to the eateries along the back wall.

Drake went with a basic turkey sandwich. Beth chose a loaded breakfast burrito, blamed it on the pregnancy.

Drake paid for both.

Through the roiling tangle of undergrads around them, they found a table in the back and settled in. The entire time, Beth smiled and looked pleasant. Drake tried to keep from asking one of the hundred questions running through his mind.

"So, uh, congratulations," Drake said. He motioned to her baby bump with one hand. Spread mustard on his sandwich with the other.

Beth ignored the question, pretended to bend over and inspect her burrito. "Thank you so much for meeting me," she hissed.

"Why are we whispering?" Drake asked.

"Because they might be listening," Beth said. Just as natural as can be, she cut her burrito in half and lifted one side to her mouth.

"Who?"

"I'm so sorry for contacting you. I didn't know who else to call," Beth said. Took a bite. Chewed, tried to keep her glassy eyes from giving way to full blown tears.

Drake left the sandwich open in front of him. "Beth, what is going on? You're cousin grabs me coming out of court yesterday, sends me to a website? I come here and find you pregnant and talking about being followed?"

"I know," Beth whispered. "It's all so awful. I can't believe I'm in this mess. I don't even know if there's anything you can do..."

"Stop apologizing," Drake snapped. He waited for Beth's eyes to meet his. "Make it make sense."

Beth nodded, motioned towards his sandwich. "Okay, but you have to eat. We have to make this look natural."

Eyes narrowed, Drake did as she said. It was tasteless as he focused on her. Waited for an explanation.

"I know it's been a while since we spoke, so I'll just pretend you know nothing about me and start at the beginning," Beth said. Another bite of burrito. Scrambled eggs falling to the tray in front of her.

"I am Missoula born, raised by my mother. Father passed when I was an infant, mom never remarried."

"Okay."

"About a year and a half ago, she got sick. Like, *really* sick," Beth continued. "Pancreatic cancer. Spent eight months in and out of Missoula County Hospital. The last couple months were a lot more in than out."

"I'm sorry to hear that," Drake said. Still forcing himself to eat. Realizing how little they had interacted the last couple of years. "You never mentioned anything. Is she okay?"

Beth shook her head. "No. She didn't make it."

"I'm very sorry," Drake repeated.

"Before she got sick, I was working for the Missoula County Credit Union. Nothing fancy, but it paid the bills. When she got sick, I had to take a leave of absence. Between that and the hospital stays..."

"The family ledger went from black to red in a hurry," Drake prompted.

"Blood red," Beth said. "At that point, it was just mom and I. No rich relatives, no real assets of any kind. The hospital wrote off most of the expense for charity, but I was still left with about fifteen thousand in expenses."

Drake took another bite. He had no idea where this was going. Wanted to press her on it, but decided to let it ride.

"After the funeral, I was a wreck. Big stack of bills. No money coming in. Then, a visitor showed up one day."

The sandwich stopped halfway to Drake's mouth. "A visitor?"

"Keep eating," Beth said. Her eyes darted about as she did the same. "One night I was sitting on the couch and a woman showed up. Nice lady. Well dressed, clean-cut. Said she worked at MCH and had heard about my situation. Wanted to make me an offer."

"For?"

Beth motioned to her stomach. "This. Claimed she knew of a family that was looking to have a baby and needed a surrogate. Said if I met with them and agreed to do it, my fee would be enough to cover the remaining bills and get my feet back under me."

"So you did it," Drake said.

"Yes, but it wasn't that simple. I met with the parents two or three different times. Talked to the doctor that would be handling the procedure. Everything. They even had an attorney draw up an official looking contract."

Drake nodded. "So this is a contract dispute? Something has gone wrong and you need me to take a look at it?"

Again Beth's eyes glassed over. "You have no idea how much I wish it were that simple."

She paused and took another bite of burrito. Forced it down as a tear slid from her eye.

"The second I signed the contract, everything changed. Part of the contract was I was given a place to stay. Turns out in a bunkhouse with about a dozen girls. All either pregnant or having just given birth."

Drake's eyes widened.

"Constant supervision," Beth continued. "That nice lady that came to see me suddenly turned into Hitler. Monitored everything we did. Who we talked to. What we ate."

"What?" Drake asked, made a face. "What in the world did you sign on to?"

Beth shook her head. Her lip quivered. "I didn't know until it was too late. I swear to God I didn't know."

Drake waited for her to regain her composure.

"What I soon realized was I wasn't just acting as a surrogate. I was involved in a ring. A ring of people that find poor, single, unattached females like myself and offer them the one thing they don't have."

"And in exchange, they get healthy vessels to serve as surrogates," Drake thought out loud.

Beth nodded. "And the girls are given peanuts."

"Who are the fathers?"

Beth shrugged. "The second it's born, the mother is cut loose. Child Services takes the child, the mother disappears."

Drake thought back to the hearing just the day before. Felt bile rise in the back of his throat.

"Disappears?"

Beth nodded. "Most of the girls, pretty much all of them, aren't from around here. Once their job is done, they go back I guess."

Dozens more questions sprang to mind. Drake ignored them. "And the girls just allow this to happen?"

"Like I said," Beth continued, "they watch us constantly. And believe me, the people they have watching aren't the kind you ever want to cross. Most of the girls are too scared, too poor, too *irrelevant* to ever speak out."

"So how are you here now?"

Beth shook her head. "They don't lock us up. There's too many to do that. Somebody would notice. But they restrict us from ever using a car, put the fear of God in us about what would happen if we ever tried anything.

"I have no doubt I'm being watched now."

Drake leaned back in his chair. Wanted to look around and see who was watching. Fought the urge.

Over half the sandwich remained in front of him. Any trace of appetite was gone.

So many questions. So very few answers.

"So why come to me?" Drake asked. "I'm a law student, I'm not a police officer."

"I know..." Beth said. "But I can't go to the police. I have no idea who all is involved in this, but it's big."

Drake leaned forward, rested his elbows on the table. He stared down at his sandwich. Shook his head. "Beth, I'm sorry. I am. I don't know much about this stuff, but it sounds awful.

"At the same time, I'm not sure what all I can do. You need law enforcement. You need protective custody. I'm not even a full attorney yet."

"I know," Beth whispered.

"I mean, I'm happy to make a few phone calls. Talk to some people, but..."

Beth's head shot up. Her eyes flicked around the room. "No. Don't. You can't tell anyone we've had this conversation."

"Okay, okay," Drake said. "Calm down."

With quick movements, she balled her burrito into its wrapper. "I should be going. I shouldn’t have bothered you."

"Wait, don't be like that," Drake said. "It's not that I don't want to help."

"I know," Beth said. "There's just nothing you can do."

She leaned down and gave him another one-armed hug. "Thank you for meeting with me. For buying me lunch."

"Please, don't go," Drake replied.

Beth pulled back, eyes again wet. "I have to."

Just like that she was gone. Behind her sat a very confused Drake and a half-eaten turkey sandwich.

Chapter Fourteen

Notch lowered the binoculars.

Smiled.

A self-satisfied smile that managed to display two things at once. His stained, dirty teeth, and his rotten soul.

He watched Beth Haggerty waddle out of the front door of the Food Zoo. Head towards the bus stop on the corner.

She had told them she was making a library run. He'd been told to keep an eye on her anyway.

Notch watched as a bus pulled up and Beth climbed in. He leaned back the driver's seat in the front of his truck and waited as it slid on past him.

Grabbed his cell-phone and thumbed it on.

One ring.

"You spot her?" the same thin, nasal, female voice asked.

There were very few people on the planet that talked to Notch in such a pointed manner. Given what she was paying him, he had no problem letting her be one of them.

Besides, they both knew it was all a front for the girls. Everybody in the organization was scared shitless of him.

The moment her tone crossed from a front to disrespect, he would put an end to it.

"Yeah," Notch said. "She made a trip over to campus. Had lunch with some guy."

"Who?"

"I don't know. He wasn't wearing a nametag."

Silence was the only response.

"He looked young. Not a professor type. They hugged like old friends when he showed up."

"How long was she inside?"

Notch glanced at the dash. "Twenty-three minutes."

"Did they leave together?"

"Nope."

More silence.

"You want me to stay on him?"

"No," the female said. "I want you to stay on her. Catch up with her. Have a little chat."

The smile grew wider on Notch face. "Make an example of her?"

"*No!* Remind her that these little field trips of hers won't be tolerated, but under no circumstances risk the health of the baby."

Notch steamed. He did not appreciate being snapped at. This bitch had no idea how close she was to offending him.

"So keep it cosmetic?" he pushed out through gritted teeth.

"Yes. And try to do it before she gets back. I'd like the other girls to see what happens when they go off-script."

"Without having to witness it," Notch said. "Got it."

A moment of silence passed.

"You know what?" the female said. "Don't. Don't touch her or even talk to her. She's in her eighth month. The Berg's are paying too much for that baby to risk anything."

Notch' eyes bulged. "So we let her walk on this?"

"Doesn't she have family?"

The sadistic smile returned. Fast. "She has that cousin."

"Yeah," the female said. "Don't put her in the hospital. Damned sure not the morgue. But let Beth know we disapprove."

"With pleasure," Notch said.

The female grunted softly, but said nothing. Ended the call without further acknowledgement or instruction.

Notch tossed the phone onto the passenger seat and eased out onto the street. He wasn't quite known for his self-restraint, but something told him this was still going to be fun.

Chapter Fifteen

There are two types of cowboy boots.

The western, or as most old-timers preferred to say, the classic, and the roper.

Both are made from calfskin. Both have a heel for riding.

The similarities stop there.

The classic uses a much higher boot shaft that stops below the knee. It features a pointed toe and curved heel, both for ease of use in the saddle.

The roper is a much shorter boot, stopping just past the ankle, some even featuring laces. It has a much shorter heel, which is squared off, and a rounded toe.

To Sheriff Spore, ropers are an abomination to everything Montana stands for.

Rather hypocritical when considering that he himself hasn't been on a horse in ages. Has never ranched. Stopped hunting years ago.

Yet, by Montana logic, if a man has a mustache and boots, he is a cowboy.

Sheriff Hardy Spore may not believe in a lot of things after twenty years as Sheriff of Missoula County, but he damn sure believes in Montana logic.

The wooden heels of his western style boots clacked loudly against his desk as he settled his feet atop it. Leaned back in his chair. Dropped his tan Stetson hat to his knee. Laced his fingers behind his head.

Three o'clock on Friday afternoon. The mess at the Meigs barn was taken care of. The Griz season opened tomorrow.

Quitting time was just a couple of hours away.

Despite his trim, hardpan appearance, Spore was a man old beyond his years. Twenty-five years working in law enforcement, even in a place like Missoula County, were taking their toll.

Already he found himself letting things slide that a decade before would have demanded his attention. Found himself eyeing the sofa on one wall in his office each afternoon with more longing.

He unlaced his fingers and extended his right hand to his desk. Latched onto the bottle of old-style RC Cola he just brought from the fridge. Popped the cap against the corner of the desk.

The soda was half way to his mouth when the phone rang in his office. Not his dispatch line, calling to let him know someone had just a hit deer or smashed a mailbox.

Not even his cell-phone.

The cell-phone. The phone that only had one number in it. No name attached.

Spore's mouth went dry. Odds were they were just calling to make sure the barn situation was under wraps.

Still, he hated every time that phone rang. Hated even more that he had to carry it at all.

"Sheriff Spore," he answered. More for anybody outside his office that might be listening than the caller. They knew he was. Wouldn't be calling otherwise.

"Head's up," the same female voice said to him. Thin and nasal. Seemed to grate his nerves every time. "We might have another situation for you soon."

"Soon?"

"Soon." No further explanation.

Spore lowered his feet to the floor. Circled his desk. Pushed his office door shut.

"Anything more concrete? And what type of situation?"

"I can't answer either one," she said. "I don't know."

"Then why are you calling me?" He was irritated. Tried not to let it show.

Too much.

Still, she picked up on it. "I'm calling to tell your lazy ass that you might actually have to earn the enormous retainer we send you every month. That going to be a problem?"

"No ma'am," Spore said. He wasn't afraid of her. She didn’t even come to his shoulder.

The people that often accompanied her frightened the piss out of him.

"I was just hoping you might have a little bit more information for me to work with. It would be helpful."

"Again, I don't have any," she said. A bit of the edge was gone. "This is a courtesy call, nothing more."

"Notch?" Spore asked. He closed his eyes as he asked. Hated even saying the name.

"Yes. About an hour ago I told him to pay someone a visit. He was told not to harm her beyond repair, but you know how he can get sometimes."

Spore thought back to the mess in the barn.

"I think we all do," Spore whispered. "Thank you for the warning."

The line was already dead.

Spore exhaled and flipped the phone closed. Went back to his chair, ran a hand through his short cropped hair.

Quitting time had just gotten a lot further off.

Chapter Sixteen

Patricia Harken slumped into the patterned office chair and rubbed her eyes. The chair gave the appearance of being padded, but was hard as a rock.

Fitting, all things considered.

Across from her, Dr. Schievers sat and rubbed his eyes as well. His desktop computer told him it was Friday afternoon, but it didn't matter.

Every day just seemed to meld into one unending marathon. Each one as tedious and demoralizing as the one before.

"How the hell did we end up here?" Dr. Schievers asked. He didn't remove his hand from over his eyes. Didn't even look at Harken as he asked it.

As vague as the question was, Harken knew what he meant. "I don't know."

The thing is, she did know. They both did.

It had started three years earlier. Not the ring or the roles they now played in it, but the events that led them to it.

At the time, Harken was a recent widower. Alone. Tired. Depressed.

Dr. Schievers was going through the motions of a marriage that had been dead for almost a decade. He and his wife put on the face and made the rounds about town, but it ended there. Separate bedrooms. Separate vacations. Separate lives.

The first time they met was through a situation similar to what they now did for the ring.

A single, teenage mother gave birth to a child nobody wanted. Dr. Schievers delivered the baby, called child services. Harken picked up the phone. Came by the next day to sign the documents.

One minute they were discussing the welfare of the child. The next they were shoving papers from his desktop to the floor. The very same desktop that now sat between them.

The fling lasted less than a year. Both sides saw the inherent foolishness in what they were doing. Decided to end things.

By that time though, the damage was done.

Or rather, the pictures were taken.

Once the conglomerate had a stack a photos that could bury them personally and professionally, neither one had a choice. They were forced to take part.

They both tried to fool themselves and say they were in it for the money. Both knew that was bullshit.

They were in it because they had no other choice.

"You think it will ever end?" Harken asked.

Dr. Schievers dropped his hand to his side. Shook his head. "I don't know how it would. It would take something pretty big to make them pull out of this. You know how much money they're making on this baby alone?"

"I heard three hundred grand," Harken whispered.

"At least," Dr. Schievers said. "They give the girl's a small piece. Grease our pockets. They're still making a killing. Several million dollars a year in cash, easy."

"Where do they find these people?" Harken asked. "The average income in Missoula is what? Twenty-eight thousand?"

"Twenty-six," Dr. Schievers corrected. "Whoever they are, they definitely aren't local."

Harken chewed the idea in silence. "Meaning we're probably not the only place they're doing this."

"Probably not," Dr. Schievers said. Resignation in his voice.

He gave another sigh and leaned forward. Slid some paperwork across the desk.

"Standard forms, you know the drill. One is the official release from the hospital to Missoula County. The other is the full acknowledgement that the baby left with a clean bill of health. Will return for all regular check-ups, to be performed as charity care by the hospital."

Harken pulled them towards her. Signed her name by the yellow tabs without even reading the forms.

This was their fourth transfer of the year already. She knew what they said.

"You taking him straight out from here?" Dr. Schievers asked.

A look of sadness passed over Harken's face. "You know, more than once I've thought about that. Thought about what would happen if I just jumped on I-90 and took off.

"East for Billings. West to Seattle. It wouldn't matter. Just...took off."

"And?"

"And every time I do, I come back to the same images in my mind. Images like what Notch did to that girl in the barn. I see myself hanging there. Or worse, I see what he would do to the baby.

"So, I stay. And I deliver the kid there. Deposit the checks when they arrive every month. Try to pretend it isn't killing me inside."

Dr. Schievers nodded. "I vacillate between shame and anger. Try to tell myself the kids are going to a better place.

"End of the day though, I cash the checks some as you do."

Harken nodded. Slid the papers off the desk and deposited them into her briefcase. Rose to leave.

"Any idea when the next one will be here?"

"Two weeks. Three at the most."

Another sad nod. "I'll see you then."

Dr. Schievers waited until she was outside the office, already half way to the nursery, before he replied. "I'll see you then."

Chapter Seventeen

Few things in the world match the excitement of a college town on football Saturdays.

And make no mistake, Missoula is most definitely a college town.

As a point of reference, the town itself totals somewhere around forty-five thousand people. Another twenty or so populate the surrounding County.

Washington-Grizzly Stadium holds over twenty-five thousand. It has been sold out for years on end. Regardless if the Griz are playing Yellowbud Tech or Montana State, one in three people in the area are showing up to see it.

Among those getting ready for the game was the Zoo Crew.

When most people in the country say they are getting ready, they mean they are picking out their favorite team apparel to wear. In Montana, those choices are made the night before.

Getting ready means they are on hand at eight a.m. game day to start tailgating.

A few years before, the Crew had considered staging their own tailgate. They entered into the lottery for a parking spot, lugged everything downtown, put on a spread for any fellow fans that wandered by.

That lasted exactly two games. They fast discovered that the effort far outweighed the rewards.

More important, Drake and Kade both realized that it chewed into their ability to get inside and watch the games.

A mortal sin if there ever was one.

Instead, the Crew used their various affiliations to roam the grounds. They'd start at the law school tailgate for appetizers. A few beers for Kade.

After twenty or thirty minutes of awkward conversation with the law students, they'd head to one put on by a group of fire jumpers.

Here they greeted Kade like a conquering hero. Welcomed the Crew. Pushed food and libations on them by the handful.

Around eleven, the group matriculated over to the Saint Michael's tent so Sage could put in her requisite face time. It was the one the entire group was always a little unsure of.

Best food, worst people.

Not only were they as backward as the law students, but many wanted to relive the glory days with Drake and Kade. Not an enjoyable experience for anyone.

To date, fourteen minutes was the longest they'd ever stayed.

From there, the schedule became more of a toss-up. If the group was still hungry, Ajax led them to the business school tailgate for Jambalaya and beers. If not, they roamed the grounds for a few minutes until kick-off.

Today, given the warmth and twelve o'clock start, they opted against the business school.

"I'm thinking we go visit the Deltas," Kade said to open negotiations. "They always have a good spread."

"Yeah, of young, blonde airheads," Sage said.

"Okay, the Kappas," Kade retorted.

"Oh yay, Kappa-Kappa-Fake Tanner. Sign me up," Sage deadpanned.

"We could always go back to the fire jumpers," Ajax suggested. "I could go for another Moose Drool before we head in."

"I'm always up for another beer," Kade agreed. "Drake?"

Drake stood on the corner outside the stadium and looked around at the sea of maroon and silver. "You know, I'm going to run and hit the head before kickoff."

"You've got to be kidding me," Kade said. Heavy eye roll.

Ajax shook his head in disapproval. "Kid went home to Tennessee and backslid on us. All there is to it."

"I'll meet you back here in fifteen," Drake pressed. Didn't even acknowledge Ajax' statement. "Still be inside long before kickoff."

Ajax continued to shake his head in mock disgust.

Kade feigned indignation for a moment. Shook his head in disbelief. "Sage? Do you need to visit the little girl's room too?"

Sage cracked a smile. "I was thinking about it, but after that comment I think I can wait. We'll see you back here in fifteen."

Drake disappeared before any of them had a chance to make another comment. He had no doubt they were firing them at his back as he retreated, but could care less as he wound a path through the crowd.

Ignorance is bliss, that kind of thing.

The door to the law school was locked to keep drunken tailgaters out and he had to use his school ID to get in. Once inside, the revelry of the outside world fell away.

What was just moments before bright sunlight and boisterous sound was now subdued lighting and stony silence.

Drake looked in either direction down the empty hallways and wound his way to the men's room. Stepped inside and unloaded the two beers he'd had that morning.

A thought occurred to him as he exited. He checked his cell-phone to find he still had ten minutes, ducked down the stairs to the basement.

To his surprise, the building wasn't as empty as it seemed. The light from the clinic office was on, the door open. A torrent of Latin music played out softly into the hallway.

A smile tugged at one side of Drake's face. There was no way those tunes belonged to Greg or Wyatt.

"Good morning," Drake said. His voice preceded him into the room.

In the back corner, Ava jumped several inches from her seat. Pressed a hand to her chest. Turned with a huffy expression on her bright red cheeks.

Her right hand shot out and killed the music.

"Good morning."

"Don't turn the music off because of me," Drake said. Slid down into his own chair. "Won't be here but a minute."

"I...I thought I was alone," Ava managed.

"No worries. Like I said, just stopping by. Besides, I happen to like Shakira."

Ava's jaw dropped. Just as fast, she recovered. "I was going to e-mail you and let you know you left your laptop here, but realized you wouldn't get it because your laptop's here."

Drake chuckled. Waved a hand at her. "I always leave it here. I don't like taking work home."

"Seriously?"

"If you saw my home you'd understand," Drake said. Kept his eyes on his computer. Checked his e-mail, rolled his head to face her. "I live with an attention-needy bulldog and a video game programmer. It would be futile for me to try."

Ava nodded, pretending to understand. It was clear she didn't.

"You're not going to the game?" Drake asked.

She had already let it be known what she thought of Missoula and every resident there. He didn't need to cement himself in that category for her.

"Uh, no," Ava said. Supreme disinterest. "I ran by that field you guys call a stadium the other day. Not worth the effort."

Drake smirked. "So you're a Saturday night in Death Valley girl, huh?"

"Geaux Tigers," Ava said. Small smile.

Drake pulled his attention back to the computer. Noticed that the discussion board from the day before was open. Clicked on it.

"You realize this makes us mortal enemies, right?" he said.

Ava arched an eyebrow. "Why's that?"

"Go Vols."

He smiled, waited for her response.

Just as fast it slid from his face. There was a new message in the discussion thread.

"You're one of *those,*" Ava said. She crinkled her nose in distaste. Offered her best disgusted face.

"Guilty," Drake said. Already his voice was distant. A small boil settled in his stomach.

He clicked open the message.

Hey, I know it's last second, but would you happen to have any extra tickets for today's game? Very desperate. In dire need of assistance.

Drake's mouth went dry. He felt his phone vibrate against his hip. Knew who it was. Didn't bother to pick it up.

"Hey, you okay?" Ava asked. "You look like someone just kicked you in the groin."

Drake tried to work his dry tongue around his mouth. "Uh, yeah. I think so."

"You think so?"

Drake didn't respond to Ava. Instead, he clicked on the respond box and paused for a moment to choose the right words.

I do. I am nursing a sick friend this morning. Do you still need them?

He hit send and waited. Could feel Ava's questioning look on him. Did not acknowledge it in any way.

In his pocket, his cell-phone buzzed against his hip. He ignored it.

Same people wanting the same thing.

The reply came less than a minute later.

Yes! Can you meet us at 601 Kent? Right off of campus?

Drake clicked out of the forum and rubbed his hands over his face. He had been sweating without realizing it.

"Are you going to be here all afternoon?" he asked.

Ava looked a question at him. "I don't know. As long as it takes I guess."

Drake grunted. Leaned forward and scribbled his phone number on a scrap of paper. Tore it off and extended it to her.

"Can you do me a favor later? Before you go, call me?"

Ava reached out, accepted the paper. "Um, why?"

"I'm very sorry," Drake said. He was already moving for the door. "I don't have time to explain right now. Just, please."

Ava sighed. "Okay."

"Thank you," Drake said.

Fifteen seconds later he was back outside, fighting his way through the crowd.

Chapter Eighteen

The Crew threw their hands up in the air as Drake approached. Mock exasperation, mixed with just a bit of real annoyance.

"Bout damn time," Kade said.

"Longest piss I ever seen," Ajax agreed.

Drake ignored them both. Leveled his gaze on Sage. "I need your help."

Kade and Ajax both laughed in unison.

"What, you forget how to work a zipper?" Ajax asked.

Sage smiled at their commentary. "What's going on?"

"Please," Drake said. His voice was low. The amusement faded at once from the group. "I need your help."

This time Sage was serious. "What's going on?"

"You remember the girl? That's pregnant? She messaged me again. Said she needs to meet and it's urgent."

"What kind of help?" Ajax asked.

"I responded back, made an allusion to nursing a sick friend. She jumped all over it. I think she might be hurt."

Around them the place was alive with pre-game festivities. Tons of locals all dressed in Griz gear, pushing their way towards the stadium.

None of the four paid them any mind. The excitement of the first game was gone.

"What can we do?" Kade asked.

Drake opened his mouth to respond. Closed it just as fast. Shook his head. "I don't know. I don't even know if we can help. She gave me an address though. I'm going to go take a look."

"You want us to come with you?" Ajax asked.

Drake weighed the offer. Shook his head. "You guys go on in. This might be nothing. If anything at all comes up suspicious, I'll call."

Kade extended a fist. "You better."

Drake met it. Did the same with Ajax.

Together he and Sage set off in the opposite direction. At just ten minutes before kickoff, most of the crowd had already moved past them. The rest was clustered around their respective tailgates.

They weren't going anywhere for the next few hours.

"Thank you for doing this," Drake said.

"Yeah, cause you know how much I hate to miss a football game," Sage said. Over dramatic eye roll to hammer home the sarcasm.

Drake smirked. "Still, thanks."

"Don't thank me," Sage said. "This is how we roll, remember?"

Drake considered heading for his car a few blocks away, thought better of it. Instead he led Sage on a diagonal pathacross campus, straight for Kent Street.

Walking at a quick pace, it took them just under fifteen minutes. Almost all of it was spent in total silence.

The entire time Drake fought with what he might soon find. He was half afraid to wonder what Sage was thinking beside him.

They found 601 Kent easy enough. Single story ranch done in brick. Couple of aspen trees in the yard. Front hedge that could use a little shaping.

No lights or visible signs of life.

"Stay here," Drake said. He left Sage ten feet back from the front door. Scaled the three steps up to the door and knocked.

No response.

Tried the doorbell, heard it echo through the house.

Still, no response.

Knocked a third time and paused. When there still wasn't a sound from within, he tried the handle. It turned in his hand. Made a small screech as the door cracked open.

"I'll be right back," he said over his shoulder. Disappeared inside.

The interior of the house was just as desolate as the outside. A tidy living room featured a sofa, armchair, flat screen television. All sat untouched.

Not a single light was on as Drake stepped through. Natural light wafted in through the curtains. Sent a ghostly pallor over everything.

"Hello? Beth? Are you in here?" Drake called.

For the first time it occurred to him that he had no idea what he was walking into. Beth had mentioned they might be watching.

Who was *they*? Were they watching?

The hairs stood on end at the nape of Drake's neck. He stepped from the living room into the kitchen. Grabbed up a knife from the drying rack by the sink.

Kept walking.

"Beth?" he said again. This time, softer.

The floor creaked beneath his feet as he came upon an empty bathroom. An empty bedroom that had been converted to a study.

He kept the knife gripped in his hand. Pushed further down the hallway. Focused his eyes on the last door ahead of him.

It was closed tight.

He stepped up to it and rapped softly with the back of his hand. "Beth?"

Tried the knob. Pushed it open a few feet.

The coppery smell of blood filled his nostrils. Every alert mechanism in his body jolted alive.

The trail began on the cream carpet just inside the door. At first just a few droplets. Dried hard and black on the ground.

As it moved forward, the trail got heavier. Much, much heavier.

The path ended at the foot of a bed. On it was a single person, lying face up. Her eyes were closed. Almost every square inch of the cream-colored blanket beneath her was stained with dried blood.

Same for the sundress she was wearing.

Drake made a face. Even at the sight of all the blood, one thing jumped out at him more than any other.

"Ella?"

Chapter Nineteen

Whoever had worked Ella over knew what they were doing.

The wounds were all superficial. Designed to draw blood. Leave a mark. Not doing any lasting damage.

Or, as Sage surmised while she worked, put Ella in the hospital.

The moment Drake found the breath in his chest, he'd called for her from the front steps. She was by his side in three seconds flat. If she was at all taken aback by what she found, she didn't show it.

Instead, she operated with cool precision. Sent Drake after some things from the kitchen. Immediately cut away the bloody dress. Did an inventory of the injuries.

Despite appearances, Ella was alive.

Sage deduced that someone had tortured her. Used some form of water punishment mixed with delicate knife work. Made the blood loss look a lot larger than it was.

Made the agony much worse on Ella.

While Sage worked, Drake scanned the scene as best he could. Every impulse in his body told him to call the police. Still, the words of Beth the day before kept him from doing it.

Just the mere mention of them had sent her into a panic. What if somebody really was watching?

From what Drake could tell, the bastard had worked Ella over somewhere else. Brought her back to the house. Staged the room so she would be found in a compromising position.

In short, she was set up as an example.

Once Sage got her cleaned up, dressed, tucked away in bed, she turned to Drake. Until that point, she had not asked a single question.

"She's definitely not pregnant. This isn't the girl you met with yesterday."

Still not a question.

Drake shook his head. "No."

"Who is she?"

"This is Ella. The cousin that came to see me at the courthouse."

Sage nodded. Flicked her gaze to the girl lying on the bed. "There's a correlation there you know."

Drake nodded. "How bad?"

Sage kept her stare locked on Ella. "They drugged her to move her. From what it seems, she's got enough sedative in her to knock out a horse."

"So she'll make it?"

"She'll make it." Sage turned her eyes back to Drake. "But she's going to wear the scars forever."

Drake's eyes slid shut. Not a voluntary movement.

"What the hell is all this?" Sage asked. "And why do you seem to be up to your ass in it?"

"I don't know," Drake said. Opened his eyes. "Either answer. Best I can tell, the only reason I'm here is the same reason you are right now. I needed a nurse. They needed a lawyer."

Sage again looked down at Ella. "This girl doesn't need a lawyer. She needs the police. Or a pissed off boyfriend with a gun."

"I suggested the police to Beth yesterday, she got scared and ran off. And I mean *scared.* She didn't say as much, but I got the impression whatever is going on here is a lot bigger than anybody realizes."

"Is there anything you can do?"

Drake shook his head. "First things first. We need to move her. Whoever dropped her here obviously knows where she lives. They might be watching."

Sage made a face. "And take her where?"

Drake sighed. "I don't know. Our place I guess."

"Is that any safer? What if they are watching?" Sage asked.

"True," Drake said. Nodded. "Maybe a hotel? Just for a couple of days, until she's awake and I can talk to a few people. Beth. The attorney I report to."

Sage said nothing. Drake could tell she was thinking in rapid-fire succession. Was holding back to spare him.

"I know it's sloppy," he whispered. He himself needed to hear it as much as he knew Sage did. "But I'm clutching at straws here. They don't exactly prepare you for this sort of thing in law school."

"I know," Sage said. "I just wish..."

"Me too."

Drake slid his cell-phone from his pocket. Hit the first speed-dial without looking at it.

On the second ring, Kade picked up. Behind him was a cacophony of sounds from the game.

"Everything alright, brother?"

"Hey, I hate like hell to ask this..."

"We're on our way," Kade said. A moment passed. The crowd noise receded a bit. "Where are we headed?"

Drake gave him the address. Told him to bring his truck.

Chapter Twenty

In true Griz fashion, the first game of the season was against a patsy. Actually, a team so putrid it gave patsies a bad name.

By the end of the first quarter, some of the students had already started to file out. Those that hadn't yet made it in from the tailgates didn't bother.

Missoula Mayor Maria Sloan lasted until halftime.

She, along with a small staff of handlers, made the rounds before the game. Stopped by the Saint Michael's tent to say hello. Swung over to the Rotary Club to smile for a few pictures. Even met up with the League of Women Voter's just to say she did.

It was still over a year until her next election, but it was never too early to start taking advantage of opportunities.

In Missoula, nothing presented an opportunity for people to be seen quite like the Griz.

Perched in her own skybox atop the eastern side of the stadium, Mayor Sloan played the dutiful fan for two solid quarters.

Cheered each time the Griz scored. Booed whenever the refs missed a call. Feigned concern when a player was down for a few minutes.

Truth was, Maria Sloan hated football. Hated everything about it. From the obsessive nature of the fans to the orchestrated barbarism the sport encouraged.

Using the excuse of an afternoon visit to a children's home, she excused herself and took an elevator to the bowels of the stadium. From there she walked to the edge of campus and hopped into her car. Pointed it towards the Bitterroot Valley south of town.

The handlers stayed behind in the press box. If anybody important from the community stopped by, she needed to have some presence there.

More important, she wanted to make sure they were nowhere near where she was going.

Twenty minutes after leaving the stadium, Mayor Sloan pulled onto a dirt drive on the north end of the Bitterroot Valley. Long and winding, the drive took her almost a half mile from the highway.

By the time she got to her destination, the outside world had melted into the background.

Though only a couple of miles outside of town, the place was isolated. A small ranch farmhouse sat in front of her. Off to the right was a pair of bunkhouses. To the left, a barn.

Behind everything ran the Bitterroot River. Mayor Sloan could see the afternoon sun glinting off of it as she exited the car.

Without ceremony she crossed the thin swath of grass that constituted a front yard and went inside. There was no need for her to knock. The person she was here to see knew she was coming. Not that she would stop to knock otherwise.

Mayor Sloan stepped inside the front door into a foyer that split two different worlds.

On the left side was a typical home. Living room with two sofas, coffee table, television. Bedroom. Bath.

To the right resembled more of a compound. The front room was lined with television monitors, all displaying closed circuit feeds. Past it was an industrial sized kitchen where two girls were busy preparing dinner.

Both were in their second trimester of pregnancy. Avoided even looking at Mayor Sloan as she stood in the foyer.

A moment later, the woman she was there to see emerged from the bathroom. She rubbed her hands in front of her as she approached.

"Maria," she said. Extended her arms out in front of her.

Mayor Sloan returned the gesture. "Yelena."

The two hugged each other tight. Released and kissed three times in succession, alternating cheeks. The traditional Russian greeting for old friends and, in this case, family.

"How was the game?" Yelena asked. She motioned them into the living room.

"Go Griz," Mayor Sloan deadpanned. Her sister was already versed in her disdain for the entire spectacle. No need to belabor the point. "How are things here?"

Yelena sighed. Tucked her long legs up under her on the couch. Pushed her thick brown hair back behind her ears. Her sharp features twisted as she pondered how to respond.

Despite the two year disparity between them, the two could pass for twins. The only real difference between them was Mayor Sloan had a deep, rich voice that played well into the microphones.

Yelena's was thin, nasal. Endearing to those that liked her. Grating as hell to everyone else.

Which was just about everyone, period.

"They're okay," Yelena said. "We've had one girl that acted like she might go off-script a little this week, but it's been taken care of."

Mayor Sloan arched an eyebrow. "Like the last one?"

She hadn't been in the barn the weekend before to see Notch's handiwork. Didn't need to be. She'd seen it before.

"Not quite that bad. He was told to stand down a bit. Seems to have done so."

"And the girl? Was the child harmed?"

Yelena shook her head. "We didn't touch the girl or the child. But we got close enough that the point was made."

"Good," Mayor Sloan said.

Silence fell in the room. The scent of Italian food wafted in from the kitchen.

"Have I mentioned how much I hate it here?" Yelena asked.

"About a thousand times," Mayor Sloan said.

"Yet, somehow, our operation keeps getting larger."

"And so do our bank accounts. You don't seem to mind every time a check comes in."

Yelena made a face that said she wanted to protest. Thought better of it and shut her mouth. "How much longer you thinking?"

"Just until my term is up. By that time we should have a serious nest egg put back. Pull up stakes and move on."

Yelena nodded. Remained silent.

"You losing your nerve?" Mayor Sloan asked. Her eyes narrowed.

"No. Just wondering."

"I think it goes without saying you have the most important job of everyone here."

"I know that," Yelena snapped. "And believe me, nobody else ever sees this side of me. I'm just asking you, as my sister."

Mayor Sloan stared at her. A mix of surprise and disgust.

Even sisters were prone to disagreements. Theirs were becoming more frequent by the day.

Mayor Sloan rose to her feet. "I should be going. There's a post-game mixer at the Lodge I need to stop by."

"Sounds fun," Yelena said. Made no effort to stand. No effort to walk her sister to the door.

Mayor Sloan showed herself out.

Chapter Twenty-One

Even six beers down, Kade worked with impressive precision.

He and Ajax stopped by the back bedroom just long enough to see what they were dealing with before heading to the garage. Like Sage, if they seemed fazed at all they didn't show it.

Calling on three years of wilderness training, Kade grabbed everything he need for an impromptu stretcher in seconds.

An old drop-cloth. An unscrewed broom handle. A painting extension stick. A staple gun.

Drake and Ajax fell in beside him. Followed his exact orders as he constructed the stretcher. Carried it to the back bedroom as Kade pulled his truck into the alley beside the house.

Inside the bedroom, Sage took over. Secured Ella and showed them how to transfer her. Held the back door as they eased her outside. Cleared the backseat for them to load her in.

The moment they were all outside, Drake went back through. Put the house back the way he'd found it. Even returned the knife to the sink.

Pulled the bedroom door shut and locked the house behind them.

Outside, Ajax and Kade were already loaded in the bed. Sage sat behind the wheel.

"Where to?" she asked.

Drake raised his palms by his side. Shrugged. "I guess a hotel. If anybody has any ideas, I'm game to hear them."

Kade twisted his head to the side. "We can stash her on the rez. Nobody would find her there. If they did, they damned sure wouldn't touch her."

Drake weighed the suggestion. It did make sense. At the same time, he couldn't put anybody else in danger. He was already potentially opening up his friends. He couldn't risk hurting their families too.

By extension, pretty much his own family.

"No. I appreciate the offer, but we have no idea what this is. Maybe in a day or two, but right now we have to be careful."

Kade looked like he might object. Opted against it. Nodded.

"Stay in town?" Drake asked. "More witnesses, better lit. Get her out in the Valley somewhere? Maybe down to Lolo?"

"As much as the idea of being in town appeals, might not be that easy," Sage said.

"Meaning?" Drake asked.

"Meaning she's on a stretcher. Looks like an extra from a bad horror flick. We can't go parading her into the Holiday Inn on Broadway."

"Shit," Drake muttered. She was right. Things were moving too fast. He was missing key details.

Ajax stood up in the bed of the truck. "Let me ride shotgun, you get in the bed."

Drake's face went blank. "Um, okay? But we don't even know where we're going yet."

"Let me make some phone calls," Ajax said. "I got it covered."

Drake knew better than to argue. His friends were all capable people. If they said they had it covered, it was covered. He stuck a foot onto the rear tire and hoisted himself into the back.

Ajax dropped to the ground on the other side with a thud. Climbed in the front seat beside Sage.

With a rumble of exhaust, the truck was off and running.

"Any idea where he's taking us?" Kade asked. The only thing about him that still resembled the guy from the tailgates that morning was his Griz t-shirt.

Drake shook his head. "He's done a lot of business with the hotels in the area. Gaming demonstrations. Meetings. I bet he's calling in some favors."

Kade nodded. Said nothing.

Drake turned and peered through the rear window of the cab. Could see Ajax' phone pressed to his head. Sage glancing back at him in the rearview mirror.

The wind tugged at them as the truck angled north on Higgins Avenue.

Kade's hair started to blow around his face. He paid it no mind. Kept himself pressed against the rear tailgate. Nodded towards Drake with his chin.

"Hey, you're blowing up man."

How he could have heard Drake's phone over the wind and truck engine, Drake wasn't sure.

He fished it out from his shorts pocket and flipped it open. Unknown number. 225 area code.

Drake paused for a moment, tried to place it. "225 area code?"

Kade shook his head.

Drake stared at it again. Wondered if he should answer. Wondered if someone had seen them loading Ella into the truck. He hadn't given Beth his number, but that didn't mean somebody else couldn't have tracked it down.

Took a deep breath. Pushed it out. Hit the green button.

"Hello?"

"Drake?" Female voice. Familiar.

Drake sighed. "Hey Ava. Thanks for calling me."

"Where the hell are you? Sounds like you're in a wind tunnel."

Drake hunkered low against the truck bed. Cupped a hand around the phone. "That help any?"

"A little. What's going on?"

Drake paused, debated how much to divulge. He barely knew Ava. Hated the idea of dragging anybody else into the mess.

Thought about Ella in the backseat of the cab behind him. Of the uphill battle he was going to have trying to do right by her and Beth.

"It's a very, very long story," Drake managed.

"Um, alright?" Ava said. Dismissive.

The truck slowed almost to a stop. Made an easy turn into a parking lot.

Drake sat up and took a quick look around. Smiled at Kade. Of everywhere in town, they should have known this is where Ajax would take them.

"Have you ever had Firetower Pizza?" he asked.

On the other end, Ava paused. "Look, if this is you asking me out..."

"No," Drake said. More emphatic than he intended. "I am not asking you out. I have a lot to explain. It's going to take a while."

"Uhhh, I don't know," Ava said.

"Please," Drake said. "After I'm done, if you're not interested, you can walk away. No questions asked. No hard feelings."

"I mean, it's Saturday night..."

"I'll even cover your office hours. For the semester."

Drake hated making the offer, but it worked.

"Okay. I'm meeting you at the, what was it, Firetower?"

"No," Drake said. He rose from the back seat as the others piled out. "I'll text you the address in a bit."

He clicked off without saying goodbye. Her next question was no doubt going to be where they were going.

He didn't have it in him to answer.

Chapter Twenty-Two

Ajax took them to The Hawthorne. A local establishment with a sister site in Bozeman. No other locations in the world.

Situated just a mile from Missoula International Airport, it was well outside of town on the west end. The kind of place where people could fly in, conduct business, fly out.

The Zoo Crew loved Missoula. Not everyone else felt the same way.

Especially not many of the people Ajax did business with.

Sometimes, one of the clients that came was of a less-than-savory makeup. The kind that enjoyed college towns. Didn't want their wives at home to find out.

For those situations, in stepped Ajax. When he first started doing business with The Hawthorne, he told them he would pay top dollar. The insinuation was it was for their discretion as much as their accommodations.

Kind of like keeping an attorney on retainer.

It took two phone calls for Ajax to arrange a room. One to the front desk. A young girl that had just started. Tried to give him the runaround.

A second to the manager.

They had a first floor suite in the back corner long before the truck reached the parking lot.

Sage pulled the truck to a stop outside the rear entrance. Drake sent Ava the address, helped Kade carry Ella inside. Ajax went to the front desk and got the keys.

Just twenty minutes after leaving Ella's house, they were in.

The suite consisted of two bedrooms split off in opposite directions. In between was a large living room with a kitchen connected to it.

Everything was adorned in hues of red and gold. Little bits of green to break the monotony.

Drake and Kade carried Ella into the left bedroom and placed her on the bed. Sage directed them on how to unload her. Got her comfortable beneath a mound of blankets and pillows.

Once she was situated, they all retired to the living room. Closed the bedroom door behind them.

Kade let out a low whistle as he dropped himself onto the couch. "Impressive."

Drake nodded. "Ajax, I can't thank you enough."

Ajax waved off the comment. "Everybody's been playing superhero today. Figured it was my turn to chip in."

"Thank you," Drake murmured. "Only for a night or two. Until we get things figured out."

"It's taken care of. For as long as it needs to be," Ajax said. Finality in his voice.

Everybody knew pressing any further would only insult him.

Drake pulled his phone out again, checked the time. Although it felt like they had been up for days, it was just four o'clock.

"So what do we do now?" Sage asked.

"If you gentlemen don't mind," Kade said, "I'm going to check some scores."

"By all means," Drake said. His head was spinning. He had no idea what he was doing.

And he knew it.

Ajax dropped into the couch beside Kade. A moment later Oklahoma thrashing Ohio State came onto the screen.

Just like that, Kade and Ajax fell into discussing it. No mention of what had just taken place. They'd done what was asked of them. Would continue to do so.

In the meantime, they were watching football.

Drake pulled up a seat at the small kitchen dinette set. Rested his elbows on the table. Locked his fingers in front of his chin.

Sage slid into a seat across from him.

"What happens next?" she asked.

Drake considered the question. "I need to get back online. Log into that message board and contact Beth. Try to get her away so I can talk to her."

Sage nodded. "Anything else?"

"I also need to get hold of my supervising attorney. See what we can do, whether it be getting protective custody or sending someone to investigate this. Maybe set up contact with the prosecutor's office."

"What can they do?"

"Until I talk to Beth, I mean *really* talk to Beth, I don't know."

Drake wished there something more he could offer. Hated like hell that there wasn't.

He also knew Sage would see right through him if he tried to embellish even a little. Hate him like hell for trying.

A sharp knock snapped all four heads towards the door. Ajax leaned forward from his end of the couch. Behind him, Kade rose to a half-standing position.

Drake stood and reached the door in three steps. He knew who was on the other side and didn't bother checking the peephole.

He also knew she wouldn't be happy.

In one fluid movement he turned down the handle and pulled the door open wide. In front of him stood Ava, half angry, half exasperated.

"You have got some nerve, you know that?" she spat. Her voice was two levels below hysterical. She made no effort to enter.

"Please, come inside. I can explain."

"I'm not going anywhere. You can explain right now. You don't know how close I was to telling you to go to hell and driving off. The only reason I came inside was to tell you what an asshole you are."

Behind him, Drake could hear snickering.

"Again, please come inside. I can explain."

"What kind of idiot do you take me for? Sliding me your number. Having me call you. Swearing you weren't hitting on me then texting me an address to some hotel."

"Ava!" Drake snapped. He stepped aside to reveal Ajax and Kade on the couch, both grinning. Sage at the table with her jaw agape. "If you'll shut the hell up and come inside, we can explain."

For the first time, Ava noticed the other three people in the room. The anger retreated from her face, replaced by embarrassment.

She blinked several times. Lowered the finger she'd been wagging at Drake. Stepped inside.

"Didn't you say something about pizza on the phone?"

Chapter Twenty-Three

Sheriff Spore pulled up in front of 601 Kent. Parked the car along the curb. Sat inside it for a long time.

The game day traffic had long since dispersed. Now, late in the afternoon, the street resembled most everything in Missoula.

Mellow. Sleepy. Bathed in late day sun.

The call had come in as he was leaving the stadium. He pretended not to hear it. Let it go straight to voicemail.

Once he was home, he checked his messages to find Yelena's annoying voice waiting for him.

"Do me a favor. Get off your lazy ass and make sure Notch didn't kill that girl. He swears she was alive when they left last night. Judging by the effect it's had on our surrogate, I'm not so sure. 601 Kent."

No hello, no goodbye. Just a simple command.

Spore sighed, continued watching the street. He'd been elected sheriff for the first time twenty-one years earlier. In the time since, nobody else had gotten more than fourteen percent of the vote.

Taking commands wasn't something he was used to.

How he'd come to find himself in this position was something he wasn't proud of. A former Griz football player, he liked to believe he had all the angles of the sport figured out.

Liked to use those angles to turn a steady profit.

For a long time his plan worked. He used his background in football to scout the college and pro games. Call in a few wagers each weekend. Make a little extra on the side.

While maybe illegal, he didn't see the harm in it. Couldn't be any worse than the slot machines in every gas station in the state.

A victimless crime if there ever was one.

Over time, two things happened. Spore got older and the game changed.

When he played, the world was in the late seventies. Football was easy to predict. It had changed though. It was no longer a three-yards-and-a-cloud-of-dust sport. It was a speed game, a passing game.

The kind of game where anything could happen any weekend.

It didn't take long for the losses to start adding up. To cover them, his bets went up.

By the time these guys found him, he was ass deep in debt. He didn't want to even listen to their proposal, let alone take it. He had no choice though.

Worse yet, they knew he had no choice.

Now, two years later, here he sat. Outside a citizen's house on a Saturday afternoon. Stalling because he was afraid of what he might find inside.

On cue, as if knowing he needed encouragement, his cell-phone started to ring. His *other* cell-phone.

Faced with having to hear that damn thin, nasal voice again, Spore climbed out. Went in through the front door without knocking.

He wasn't sure what he might find inside. Touched the service gun on his hip every few seconds. Felt sweat rise on his back.

One by one he checked each of the rooms. Found nothing. No signs of struggle. Not even a drop of blood.

So far, Notch was good for his word.

The last door stood closed and Spore zeroed in on it. For good measure he pulled the Glock out, held it in his left hand. Pushed the door open with his right.

The smell of blood and mildew made his eyes water. He coughed twice as he stepped inside. Followed the path of darkened blood spatter on the floor.

In total, he spent ten seconds in the bedroom.

In rapid fashion, he jammed the gun back in its holster and went outside. Left the front door unlocked. Climbed into his car and dialed Yelena.

"Bout damn time," her voice rasped.

"We've got a problem," Spore said. Ignored her comment.

"I'm tired of you starting every conversation that way."

"I'm tired of having to clean up your messes."

The words were out before Spore realized he was saying them. His eyes snapped shut. He pushed his breath out through his nose. Waited for the vitriol that was coming his way.

Instead, Yelena asked, "He killed her, didn't he?"

"I...I don't know," Spore replied.

The line was silent for a moment.

"What do you mean, you don't know?" Low voice. Measured words.

"I mean, I don't know. There's a ton of blood for sure. No body."

Spore could hear a sharp intake on the other end of the line.

"I'll call you back."

Chapter Twenty-Four

Beth Haggerty shoved pizza into her mouth like she hadn't eaten in days.

She was perched against the headboard of the bed in the opposite bedroom of Ella. Pillows buffeted her oversized body.

Ava sat beside her. One leg perched on the bed, the other foot planted on the floor.

Sage leaned against the doorframe with her arms crossed.

Drake sat on the desk in the room, his legs swinging free beneath it.

Ajax and Kade continued to watch football in the living room.

After Drake got Ava inside, he commandeered her laptop and went to GoGriz.com. Sent a message asking if Beth and her boyfriend wanted to swing by an after party off-campus.

Beth's response came back within three minutes.

Ava took him to grab his car while he filled her in on what he knew. She seemed skeptical of everything he said, but went along with it anyway.

Drake wasn't sure if it was the sight of Ella or morbid curiosity that compelled her to do so.

He picked Beth up at the Food Zoo. Dropped her off at Albertson's. From there Ava picked her up and took her to Wal-mart. One more transfer to Sage, who brought her to The Hawthorne.

Ava pulled in a minute later. Drake another after that, a stack of pizzas in his hands.

The first order of business was to show Ella to Beth. Her reaction was as to be expected.

Violent crying followed by hysterical anger.

Once they assured her Ella was okay, she started to calm down. Everyone else attacked the pizza while she sat and stared into the distance.

About the time Kade turned the television to USC and Hawaii, she came around. Began speaking again.

Started to eat. And eat.

When everybody was done, Drake and the three ladies retired to the spare bedroom.

Beth kept eating. Her eyes were glassy, cheeks red.

"I'm sorry," she said. "This is just so damn good. They watch what we eat out there, like a slice of pizza might hurt the baby or something."

"Aren't pregnant women prone to crazy food cravings?" Ava asked. "That must be hard."

"You have no idea," Beth confirmed. "I have been dying for mint chocolate chip ice cream. The closest thing I ever get is graham crackers."

Drake made a face. He didn't know much about being pregnant, but that sounded like a poor trade-off.

"Beth, please keep eating, but do you mind if we ask you some questions?"

She nodded. Shoved half a slice in her mouth. Mopped her face with a washcloth.

"Now, before we do this, let me say you are safe here," Drake said. "Nobody is watching and nobody is coming. This can't be like last time. You need to talk to me here."

Beth finished chewing. Swallowed. Nodded.

"Let's start with Ella. You told me it was just you and your mom. How is it you have a cousin here? Is there more family around?"

Drake had filled in Ava earlier on his prior conversation with Beth. Sage had now heard it twice.

Beth shook her head. "Ella isn't my cousin. She was my roommate the first part of college. Before I moved back home to take care of mom. We just came up with that so I didn't seem quite so...alone."

"Make them think there was family nearby. Somebody checking on you," Drake thought out loud.

A tear slid down Beth's face. "Lot of good that did."

"Why would anybody hurt her? Did she try to take you away? Was she investigating them?"

Again Beth shook her head. "They hurt her to send a message to me. After they were done with her, they took a bunch of photos. Brought them to me. Told me it was only the start, that they'd kill her and make me watch if I tried anything else."

"Anything else?" Drake asked.

"Like meeting with you," Beth whispered.

Drake's eye narrowed, a sigh slid out. He turned his head, met Sage's gaze.

They knew who he was. What he might represent for them.

In her fear, Beth's floundering was pulling more and more people into the deep end with her.

"I bet they're going crazy now," Beth said. "I was supposed to be going for eggs."

"I can't believe they let you out at all," Ava said.

"After they showed me the pictures earlier, I was a wreck. I don't think they believed I would try to meet with anybody again."

"If they monitor you, how have you been communicating with me?" Drake asked. "I can't believe they give you guys open internet access."

Beth pulled an iPhone from the pocket of her hooded sweatshirt. Held it up and wiggled it in the air. "It's Ella's. She slid it to me a few days ago. They don't know I have it."

"How many are *they*?" Ava asked.

"I don't know," Beth said. Another head shake. "There's the woman that runs things at the house. She always seems to have a few guys around, but I don't know how many.

"Like I told you the other day, outside of that I have no idea. I know a week ago they blindfolded us, took us all out to a barn. Made us watch as they tortured a girl that had tried to get her child back."

She fell silent for a moment. A shudder wracked her body. When she resumed speaking, her voice was just a whisper.

"You should have seen the guy doing the torturing. He was a twisted bastard if there ever was one."

"Any clue who he was?" Drake asked.

"No," Beth whispered. “All I know is they refer to him as Notch. I have no idea what his real name is.

"We were all scared to death. And that was *before* he went to work on that girl. After that, we were all catatonic."

"So they killed her?" Ava asked.

"No," Beth whispered. More tears. "Just killing her would have been merciful. What they did to her was savage."

Beth's chin fell to her chest. Heavy sobbing.

Drake, Ava, and Sage all exchanged glances. None of them spoke. Waited for Beth to cry herself out.

It took almost five full minutes. When she was done, she raised her wet and blotchy face up to look at them.

"That's when I decided to find you. All along I knew what was going on was wrong, but I steeled myself to it. Told myself I would get through it, collect the money, move on. Maybe go out to the coast, start over.

"But in that moment, I knew without a doubt that it would never happen. I would never see a dime that was owed to me. And if I tried to make them pay, I would end up just like she did."

The room fell silent. After three long days, things were starting to fit together.

"So this girl," Drake asked, voice low, "she tried to make them pay?"

"Yes, but that's not why they killed her," Beth said. "What got her killed was when she went to the police."

"The cops showed up at the house and tried to arrest them?" Ava asked.

"No," Beth whispered. "The cops called the house and told them what she had done."

Chapter Twenty-Five

The clock said it was just seven. It didn't matter. Beth was exhausted.

She couldn't return to the compound. They had to know she'd been gone way too long for a simple trip to the market. It was only a matter of time before they found out Ella was gone too.

For the night, it was decided she would stay there. She offered no word of protest to the suggestion. Seemed relieved by it in fact.

Once it was mentioned, she nodded once and crawled into bed beside Ella. Even with the two of them sharing, the king sized bed swallowed them both.

Sage checked to make sure Ella was still sleeping and closed the bedroom door behind her. Kade muted the television.

All five sat in various positions around the room.

"What the hell do we do now?" Drake asked.

Nobody said anything. Ava and Sage both shook their heads.

"I mean, she just told us going to the police is what got the last girl killed," Drake said. He was thinking out loud.

The last statement by Beth had been a bombshell. Left everyone reeling.

Ajax and Kade both made faces from the couch.

"For reals?" Kade asked.

Ava nodded in response.

"What can you guys, as lawyers, do?" Sage asked.

Ava looked up at Drake. She didn't say anything, but the implication was clear.

"Not a lot," he said. "Most of what we can do is on the civil side. We can file a suit, but against who? The police? These mystery people down in the Bitterroot?"

"But they killed a girl," Sage said.

"True, but that's a criminal charge," Ava said. "And the only one that can file criminal charges is the government."

"And my guess is if the police are colluding here, so is the county attorney. You don't have one without the other, especially in a place like Montana," Drake added.

Ava smirked, shook her head. A Pavlovian response to the mention of Montana.

"So why not leapfrog the county?" Ajax said. "Go state."

Drake shook his head. "One in the same." He paused for a moment. Turned his attention to Ava. "But that's not a bad idea. Take it to the district attorney."

Ava pursed her lips. "Go to federal court with it. Interesting idea."

"Judge Denard was appointed by Clinton in '98. I find it hard to believe somebody could have gotten to him."

Everyone remained silent. Waited for him to continue.

Drake pondered the idea for another few moments. Shook himself back to the present.

"Ava, tomorrow we'll go see Lauer. Talk to him about getting us in front of the DA."

Ava checked her watch. "Why wait? It's only seven."

Drake snorted. "This is Missoula. Most of the town has been drinking since eight o'clock this morning. If he's still upright at this point, he's swaying."

Ava opened her mouth, closed it just as fast. Turned to the others. "Wait, he's serious isn't he?"

Ajax and Kade both grinned from the couch. Said nothing.

Sage made a non-committal gesture from her chair that said he wasn't wrong.

"Jesus, where the hell am I?" Ava whispered.

The rest of the room broke into a low chuckle.

Still smiling, Drake pushed forward. "That brings us to the next thing we have to consider."

"What's that?" Kade asked.

Drake motioned towards the closed bedroom door with his chin. "What do we do with them?"

"I told you, the room is taken care of," Ajax said. There was no inflection of any kind in his voice. A simple delivery of facts.

"I know," Drake said. "I mean, from what Beth was telling us, it sounds like we should have somebody around all the time. Just in case."

Kade cast a glance to Ajax. "There's three of us. We can do that."

Drake shook his head. "Again, I appreciate the offer, but we can't do that. You guys have lives. I have prosecutors to meet with."

"I know a guy," Ajax said.

"You know a guy?" Sage asked. Made a face.

"Okay, *I* don't really know him, but he's a friend of the family," Ajax said. He didn't elaborate any further. Didn't have to.

Everybody in the room, save Ava, knew the kind of wealth the Jackson family had. They also knew that didn't come without dealing with the occasional nefarious character.

"Thank you," Drake said, "but I was thinking someone a little less conspicuous. Problem is, he won't work for free."

All four stared back at him, faces blank.

"It's covered," Ajax said.

Once more, Drake shook his head. "I was thinking Rink."

Understanding spread across the faces of the Zoo Crew. Kade and Ajax both broke into broad grins.

"I retract my previous offer," Ajax said. "I don't think I can be of any help there."

Ava's face went from blank to confused. "What am I missing here? Who the hell is Rink?"

The Crew remained silent. Did their best to suppress chuckles.

"Who the hell is Rink?"

Unable to hold it back any longer, all four howled with laughter.

Chapter Twenty-Six

Tension hung in the air.

Every person in the room knew each other. Nobody said a word. Nobody even made eye contact.

One by one they'd shuffled in and took seats. Started in the back and worked their way forward.

The call had gone out at midnight. That was the pre-determined timeframe Yelena had given Notch to find Ella. When nothing turned up, she made the calls.

Told Notch to forget about Ella. Find Beth.

A few minutes before eight a.m. they'd started to roll in. Any earlier would have looked suspicious. Any later, some of them would have missed church.

This was urgent, but so was staying off the radar.

Dr. Schievers was the first to arrive. He was dressed in scrubs, even though it was Sunday and he had no intention of going into the hospital.

Harken and Spore pulled in side by side, walked in together. Neither did more than nod to acknowledge the other. They both chose chairs on opposite sides of the room.

Judge Tanner came in next. Dressed in slacks and a black cable knit, headed on to church as soon as they were done. He, like the others, had a tight grimace on his face.

Bennett was the last to arrive. He wore suit pants and a white Oxford shirt minus the tie. Looked and smelled like Saturday night had not yet ended. Kept his bloodshot eyes aimed at the floor.

Yelena waited for everyone to be seated. She stood with her arms folded in front of her at the front of the room, a frown on her face. Appeared every bit a school teacher standing over a class.

Beside her stood Mayor Sloan. Same frown and disposition.

"I think we all know why we're here this morning," Yelena said as means of an introduction.

A few heads nodded. Nobody spoke.

"And to answer your question, Notch hasn't found either of them yet."

A couple of other heads lowered themselves.

"What the hell is going on here people?" Yelena demanded.

Nobody said anything. A couple of sideways glances. Nothing more.

"Huh?" she spat. "Somebody answer me!"

Finally Bennett, in his alcohol-infused inhibition, spoke up. "Shouldn't we be asking you the same thing?"

Every head turned to him. Yelena and Mayor Sloan's eyes both bulged.

"You came to us each with a specific role," he pressed. "Dr. Schievers delivers the kids. Patricia works the Child Services side. I handle the paper work. Judge Tanner rubber stamps the proceedings. Kirby cleans up your messes."

As he spoke, others raised their eyes from the floor. Started to exchange glances.

Yelena set her jaw. Cast a glance to her sister, sent a withering glare at Bennett. "You have got some nerve, you know that?"

Bennett raised his palms to her. "Hey, I'm just saying, you guys claimed to have housing and security taken care of. That's what seems to be the problem here."

"Maybe we need to show you all again just what our security is capable of," Mayor Sloan challenged.

Bennett opened his mouth to respond, but Judge Tanner beat him to it.

"I think what Riley is trying to say is, we're all on board here. For better or worse, we're a part of this. We all know that. You don't have to convince us of anything."

"But?" Yelena pressed.

"But we're not the problem," Judge Tanner said. "The girls are. We're not the ones you need to be shaking down this morning. We don't know where they are. We sure didn't help them."

The other heads nodded around the room.

"So *I'm* the problem, is that what you're all saying?"

Nobody in the room turned towards the voice. A few cringed involuntarily. The rest remained in stony silence.

Not one of them had even heard Notch enter.

Yelena kept her arms folded across her chest. Raised her chin, stared down her nose at the group. "I kind of think that's what they're saying Notch."

Bennett raised his eyes, opened his mouth. For the first time ever, the lawyer in the group couldn't find the words.

Again Judge Tanner jumped in to help.

"Nobody is saying anything of the sort," he said. Voice low, even. "We know how many girls there are here. It would be impossible for you folks to keep tabs on that many. We're just saying, something has occurred that has started making them rethink things."

"Hmm," Mayor Sloan said.

Her sister snorted beside her. Lifted her gaze to Notch. "Anything new?"

"Not a damn thing," he hissed. "The house is empty. Nobody's even looked at it as they drove by."

"Anything else?" Mayor Sloan asked.

Notch twisted his head, glared at her. "That's the problem with picking girls off the trash heap of society. There aren't connections to follow when things go to hell."

The air went from tense to *holy shit.*

The sisters stood and stared on one end. Notch on the other.

Every single person between them tried to make themselves as small as possible.

The standoff lasted two full minutes. Notch blinked first.

"Three days ago I saw her talking to somebody on campus. Can't be a coincidence. I'll find him. He'll talk."

Not a single word held any uncertainty. Simple, declarative statements on every point.

Yelena nodded her head. Equal parts at his plan and the fact that he had spoken first.

This was the group's first real foray into the weeds. It was important the group hierarchy was still observed.

"Good. In the meantime, the rest of you keep a sharp eye and ear out. I don't think I need to remind anybody here what would happen if this girl went public."

Everyone waited a moment to make sure she was done. Stood and filed out without another word.

None of them needed reminding.

Chapter Twenty-Seven

Drake pulled his truck to a stop in front of Professor Lauer's house just shy of eleven. He parked right on the curb, made no motion to get out.

Beside him, Ava stared at the two-story home just a few blocks away from the law school. The truck engine ticked in an even rhythm.

Ava was the only one to have left The Hawthorne the night before. After she did, Kade pulled out the sofa bed and the Crew flipped for the bedroom.

Sage and Drake won the bedroom. Ajax and Kade took the sofa.

That morning, Sage drove him back to his place to check on Suzy Q and grab his truck. Kade and Ajax were still asleep when they left. Planned on staying there for the afternoon and watching more football.

Ella and Beth both slept soundly through the night.

Hair still wet, Drake was dressed in jeans and a v-neck t-shirt. Beside him, Ava wore a pencil skirt with matching pullover.

Getting better, but still a long way from Missoula-on-a-Sunday-morning.

"Wait, this is where Lauer lives?" Ava asked.

"Yup," Drake said. "You sound disappointed."

"I mean, I thought he was a practicing attorney in town? And just taught as an adjunct?"

"Yup, and yup." Drake knew already where she was going. Was going to make her say it out loud.

Ava turned and half-glared at him. "I guess I just expected something a little nicer. The attorneys where I come from all live in half-million dollar homes."

Drake leaned around her, stared at the house. It was two stories with a columned porch. Array of oak trees. Maybe a third of an acre of ground.

"Well, you have to keep in mind two key points," he said. "One, this is Missoula. The medium income here is twenty-six thousand dollars."

"You're shitting me."

Drake moved right past the comment. "Second, that *is* a half-million dollar home."

He could see Ava's eyes bulge from where she sat. "You're shitting me."

A hint of a smile tugged at his face. "Houses in the university district all go for four hundred grand or more."

"On twenty-six grand a year?"

The front door opened and Lauer stepped out. Motioned to the truck.

"Have and have-nots don't only exist in the big city," Drake said. Wrenched open his truck door and swung around the front.

Ava waited for him to join her on the sidewalk. Together they went up the front walk towards the porch.

Lauer stood in a pair of jeans and an oversized sweatshirt waiting for them. The bulk of it seemed to somehow make him appear even smaller.

The scowl on his face gave him the appearance of an angry child.

"You know, when I gave that little speech about not wanting to babysit you guys, this isn't what I had in mind," he said as way of an opening.

The early morning air was warm. Definitely not hot.

Drake was already sweating.

His two emails to Lauer the night before asking for a meeting had both gone unanswered. It wasn't until he and Ava both placed calls and left messages that he reluctantly agreed to the meeting.

He wasn't happy about it.

"We can appreciate that," Drake said. "And we're very sorry to be here under these circumstances. It's just that we're in a little over our head here."

"What about your classmates?" Lauer snapped.

Drake shook his head. "Greg and Wyatt both said to come see you."

He hated bringing his friends into it like this. Then again, what he said was true.

Lauer checked his watch. "This is my Sunday with the kids. You have five minutes."

Drake and Ava relayed what they knew in just under four. They had rehearsed it twice on the way over. Each one knew what they were supposed to say and when the other one would pick up.

In the truck it had taken right at five minutes both times.

The combination of Lauer's icy demeanor and their own nerves made for a twenty-percent decrease in time.

When they were done, both fell silent. Stared at him.

They were each short on breath from the rapid-fire debrief, but didn't dare let it show.

Lauer again checked his watch. Made a face that went from icy to Three Mile Island.

"The only thing I can see that even resembles an attorney about either one of you right now is that you stayed on time. Otherwise, I am offended that they'd even consider either one of you to be competent to practice law."

Drake's jaw dropped open. Ava went rigid beside him.

"Let me see if I have this straight. Some hard luck case let herself get knocked up for money, then had a change of heart? Believed you could help her, and is trying to get out of it?"

Drake's face betrayed his confusion. "What? No."

Lauer blew right on through it. "And then you thought you could interrupt my Sunday and I would sing your praises for being such complete idiots? That about cover it?"

Neither one said anything. They knew better than to.

Lauer kept his arms folded across his chest. Shook his head in disgust.

"There's nothing we can do. We're lawyers, not miracle workers."

Ava started to say something. Never got the chance.

"Get the hell off my porch."

Chapter Twenty-Eight

"Is it any wonder I hate this place?"

Drake sat behind the wheel in a daze. The truck was running, but he made no effort to move it.

"Huh?" he mumbled.

"Shit like that," Ava said. Her arms were folded across her stomach. She was fuming. "I should have known yesterday when you lured me to a hotel room this was all going to end badly."

The comment snapped Drake awake.

"*Lured* you to a hotel room? What, with a battered girl, a pregnant girl, and my three friends?"

"Crock of shit. Whole damn thing."

Venom welled in the back of Drake's throat. Veins bulged in his forearms as he squeezed the steering wheel. "Don't you dare blame this on me. I had no way of knowing that Napoleon-Complex-having-prick would react that way."

Ava remained silent a moment. Pushed loud breaths out through her nose. "Sorry. I've just never, and I mean *never,* been talked to like that before."

"Me neither," Drake muttered. "At least not by someone that didn't get his ass lit up for it."

Ava remained silent. If she didn't understand the football reference, she let it go just the same.

"You know what I don't get?" Drake asked.

"Why the little ones are always the biggest asses?"

"No, *that* I get," Drake said. "What I don't get is why he was so combative. He didn't listen to a word we said. We could have walked up there and said we have video of a client getting carjacked in broad daylight and he still would have shot it down."

Ava considered the idea. "Yeah, now that you mention it."

"And that couldn't have all been because we asked for five minutes of his precious Sunday could it?"

Ava shook her head. Said nothing.

Drake sighed loudly. Continued to mull the entire thing over in his head.

"You planning on letting this go?" Ava asked.

Drake continued thinking in silence. Kept his eyes trained straight ahead, his grip tight on the wheel.

"No," he said. "I don't care what that pint-sized prick says. I saw what these assholes did to Ella. How scared Beth was."

Ava nodded. "Just so we're clear, I have no interest in being a sidekick in some superhero fantasy."

Drake managed a small snort. "And just so we're clear, I have even less interest in becoming a martyr."

Ava matched the snort. "So we're on the same page here?"

Drake nodded. "We are." Offered his fist to her.

She stared at it like it was a second head.

"Never mind," Drake said. Pulled the hand back and used it to slide the truck into drive.

"So what do we do now?" Ava asked.

On the dash, Drake's phone started to vibrate. He eased the truck up to the stop sign at the end of the street and flipped it open.

Managed a small smile.

"Now, we go introduce you to Rink."

Chapter Twenty-Nine

The suite was awake and alive by the time they got there.

The bed in the living room was folded back into a couch. Kade and Ajax manned either end of it. On an armchair across from them sat Beth. Sage used a wooden chair from the kitchen table.

Every one of them was circled up around the coffee table in the middle of the room.

Standing on it was a wiry man in a black and red flannel tucked into faded jeans. Thick wool socks adorned his feet. A trucker's cap was pulled down over flame orange curls. A matching beard protruded from his chin.

Drake and Ava walked in to find him perched in a precarious position on the table. No doubt in the middle of a story. Every eye in the room trained tight on him.

He stopped mid-sentence. A smile grew across his face.

"Well if it's not the next mayor of Missoula, Montana," he said. Thick accent. North Dakota, maybe Canada.

Drake matched the smile. Stepped forward with his hand outstretched. Retracted it and embraced the man in a hug.

"I'll never be half the man your mama was," Drake said, slapping his friend on the back. He released the embrace and looked him up and down. "I see you're going with a different look these days?"

The man ran his hands down the front of his flannel shirt. "Yeah, been up in Banff the last few months. Gave up my fashion sense for something a little more efficient for the summer."

"Meaning something you don't have to wash very often?" Drake asked.

The man pursed his lips, tilted his head. "You forgot warmer. That too."

Everyone in the room laughed.

Drake stepped to the side and extended a hand towards Ava. "This is my partner Ava Zargoza. Ava, this is Rink."

Ava made a face. "Rink?"

"An unfortunate nickname," Rink said. "These guys were footballers, I was more of a hockey man."

He stepped forward and thrust his right hand towards her. Swept the cap off his head with the left. Under it his curls were formed in a deep widow's peak.

A jagged scar over two inches long ran right along the hair line.

Ava accepted the hand. Looked him up and down.

Rink made no attempt to hide his leering back at her. Without removing his eyes he asked, "So when you say she's your partner..."

"I mean she's helping me on this case," Drake said.

"But I'm just as off-limits as if we were sleeping together," Ava said. Gave him a sweet smile.

Kade and Ajax both rolled with laughter. Beth raised a hand to her face. Feigned embarrassment.

Sage shot a raised eyebrow to Drake.

Drake laughed and slapped his friend on the back. "You'll have to pardon Rink here. Poor kid doesn't have the manners the good Lord gave a dog."

Rink released Ava's hand. Gave a twist of his head. "That's not necessarily true. Depends on the breed."

Drake pulled a pair of chairs from the table and set them up facing inward. He took up a spot beside Sage. Ava settled in beside him.

Rink returned to the coffee table. Dropped down onto it.

"Rink came to Missoula the same time most of us did," Drake said. "We were here to play football, he was here to play for the junior hockey team."

"Play being a very loose term," Kade added.

"Meaning?" Ava asked.

"Meaning, I was a pugilist," Rink said.

"A thug," Ava corrected.

"It's a matter of opinion, but yes. You could say that," Rink said. "Say, has anybody taken you out to Paul's yet? Best breakfast in town."

A few more snickers from the crowd.

Ava turned to Drake. "You brought us a hockey player?"

Drake held a hand up to her. "Listen, he might not look like a whole lot, but this man's battles were legendary. Epic."

"Packed the Ice House every weekend just to watch him go," Ajax added.

"And now that your gladiating days are over?" Ava asked.

"Now I coach the team," Rink said matter-of-factly. "Spend my summers off the grid, winters in ice boxes all over the Rockies. You guys were lucky to catch my sat phone when you did."

"Oh yea, real lucky," Ava said. Added an eye roll for emphasis.

Rink looked at her, twinkle of mischief in his eye. "Hu-Hot? You like Mongolian barbecue?"

Ava glared. Shook her head. Drake jumped in before she could say anything.

"So, Rink, the reason we asked you here was to act as a security detail for us for a little while."

"Done," Rink said.

"Not for us, but for Beth and Ella. You can stay here with them as long as it takes."

"Done."

"I'll be honest, right now we have no idea what you're up against. We know of at least one sadistic bastard. Few other followers."

"Done," Rink said again. Never questioned anything. Never took his eyes from Ava.

"We'll be around to help as much as possible. Should get this figured out fast. Until then..." Drake let his voice drop off.

"Done. How about Italian sweetheart? I know a great little place down in the Valley."

Ava sighed. Shook her head. Turned to Drake. "How many shots to the head did this guy take?"

Drake smiled, shook his head. "Hey, we needed an enforcer. The man's good at what he does."

Chapter Thirty

Two sounds filled Drake's ears.

The South Fork River flowing by and Suzy Q's labored breathing.

Drake was well aware of the fact that bulldogs can't swim. Had discovered that first hand on more than one occasion over the years. At the same time though, he couldn't condone leaving her behind.

He'd missed her like hell the entire time he was gone. Had gotten to spend precious little time with her since getting back.

Per usual, his was the only automobile in the lot. During the summer it wasn't uncommon to see the Flats teeming with fisherman out for an early catch.

Now that the calendar had eased forward into September, the place was pretty much his.

Drake waited until six o'clock before climbing from the truck. Walked around to the back and dropped the tailgate.

Suzy Q followed right on his heels, a clatter of toenails on pavement. Just as fast, she disappeared into some high grass nearby to sniff around.

The only sign of her was the exaggerated breathing through her flattened nose.

With practiced hands, Drake uncased his fly rod and assembled the pieces. Threaded the thick, neon yellow line through the eyelets.

Above him, the morning sky turned from charcoal to light grey. A thin breeze pushed around the Aspen leaves in the trees lining the lot.

A single pair of low-slung headlights cut through the morning. They pulled into the parking lot and came to a stop nose to nose with his truck, headlights washing everything in harsh fluorescent light.

A moment later they blinked off and Sage emerged from the car.

"Thin crowd this morning?" she asked, climbing out.

"Am I not good enough?" Drake asked. Tied another caddis fly onto the end of his line.

Sage stood and stretched her hands high overhead. Rotated at the waist. "Didn't say that."

"Besides, I happen to not be alone," Drake said. "For the first time ever, the womenfolk have the guys outnumbered at a Zoo Crew gathering."

Sage's face fell flat. Her hands dropped to her side with a slap. "Really?"

Without looking up, Drake whistled a two-note call to Suzy Q.

A second later she burst out from the weeds, bounding as fast as her compact body would allow.

Sage coughed out a laugh. Squatted to the ground and scratched behind her ears.

"You seem surprised," Drake said.

"No," Sage said, fingers working through Q's short brown hair. "Well, maybe a little."

"Who else would I bring to out here?" Drake asked. He had a vague idea who Sage had in mind. Preferred to feign ignorance just the same.

Sage pushed herself to a standing position. "Don't play dumb. It doesn't suit you."

Drake smiled. "I'm not sure if you remember last night, but that poor girl has her hands full right now."

Sage smiled. "Rink sure is a talker isn't he?"

"When he started talking about how much he loves Mexican food, I almost lost it," Drake said.

Drake, Ava, and Sage had all gone their separate ways sometime around nine the night before. At that point, Kade and Rink were already most of the way through a case of Coldsmoke Ale.

Ajax wasn't far behind them.

They had all offered to make it out in time for fishing, but Drake waved them off. Lied and said he was going straight to the office this morning.

"How'd you know I'd be here?" Drake asked. Pulled on his waders. Closed the tailgate and grabbed up his gear.

Sage opened the backseat of her car, grabbed her stuff as well. Carried her waders under one arm. "For as light-hearted as you're playing this thing at the hotel, I can tell it's weighing on you."

"Meaning?"

"Meaning there's no way you wouldn't be here."

Drake considered trying to challenge her. Trying to tell her he is wildly unpredictable and she just got lucky.

Truth was, she was right. He let it go.

"It's...it's just. I don't know," Drake mumbled. "I've spent so damn much time the last two years pouring over case law. Sitting through lectures. Responding to inane questions.

"And I'm fast discovering it is all bullshit. Starting this summer, and continuing now, I find out that the gap between what I've been taught and what I need to know is enormous."

He fell silent. They walked together along the gravel path for the river bank. Suzy Q cut a zigzag path in front of them.

"Probably not making any sense."

Sage kicked at a rock with the toe of her shoe. "No, you are. It's kind of like reading about being a nurse in a book. Until you've been in an OR and seen the blood, you have no idea what you're really getting into."

"Right," Drake said. "This girl came to me with a problem. A huge problem. And I have no idea what to do."

"Well..."

"Check that," he said. "I've had two ideas. Go to the police and go to my supervising attorney. Neither one were right."

"That's not true," Sage said. "They were both right. The fact that they weren't just speaks to how messed up this whole situation is."

Drake exhaled. "Yeah it is. I'm flying by the seat of my pants here. Have no idea what I'm going to do next. And the worst part is,

I somehow keep dragging more and more of my friends into the mix."

The sound of the water got louder as they emerged on the gravel bar. Sat their supplies on the same felled tree.

"You'd do it for us," Sage offered.

"That's not going to help me any if something happens to one of you though."

Sage decided to change directions. “Can I ask you something?”

Drake made a waving motion with his hand. Said nothing.

“Why do you feel so compelled on this? It’s more than just wanting to help or doing your job. It’s almost like…”

“I owe her,” Drake finished. “And I do. She helped me, someone she barely knew, at a time when she had no reason to and nobody else would.”

“She brought you notes,” Sage pointed out.

“Doesn’t matter,” Drake said. “She went out on a limb to help me. I owe her the same.”

Sage started to reply. Thought better of it.

"Why don't you take point today," Drake said. "My mind's even further away than it was Friday. Not sure how much actual fishing I'll get done."

He didn't wait for a response. Just took off for a nearby eddy, Q on his heels.

Chapter Thirty-One

Monday mornings.

If there was a greater hell on earth that didn't involve wearing a tie, Drake wasn't sure what it was.

After dropping Suzy Q off at the apartment and grabbing a quick shower, he went straight to the law school. It was only eight-thirty, but that didn't faze him any.

Was a good thing even.

With luck he could avoid Lauer. Both from their interaction the day before and for what he was planning to do later on.

While the law school had started the week before, Monday marked the first day of class for the rest of campus. What just days before was a quiet and sleepy parking lot was an absolute nightmare.

Drake found one of the last remaining spots in the corner of the lot and pulled in. Grumbled to himself as he gathered his things.

Damn overeager undergrads. They were almost as bad as first year law students.

Much like the Saturday before, the interior of the law school was subdued compared to everything going on outside. Drake avoided the main lobby and cut a path down the back stairwell and into the clinic office.

To his relief, it was empty.

To his chagrin, the solace didn't last long.

Just before nine a pair of familiar voices rolled into the office with all the grace of an elephant. Both wore flip-flops on their feet, carried a mess of papers and books in their hands.

"Do you see what I see?" Wyatt asked. Drake didn't bother to turn around and look. He knew they were pointing at him.

"That...that can't be who I think it is, is it?" Greg asked.

Drake felt a finger poke into his shoulder blade.

"No, I think it might be," Wyatt said.

Drake grimaced and rotated to face his friends. "What's the good word boys?"

Both of them fell into their chairs. Left their tangle of books and papers balanced on their desks behind them.

"No good words," Greg said. Tone serious.

Drake leaned forward. "Okay?"

"Rumor mill has it you're already on the Shit List," Wyatt said.

"You and her both," Greg said. Motioned towards Ava's desk with his chin.

The news didn't come as a great surprise to Drake. The fact that it was already out did.

"Where'd you hear that from?" Drake asked.

Wyatt shook his head. "It's all over. Rumor is somebody saw you guys have a shouting match with Lauer in his front yard yesterday."

"Yelling and screaming. Quite the public spectacle," Greg added.

Drake's face hardened. "That's not at all what happened. We went to him with a case. He shot it down. Got a little pissy, but nothing like that."

Greg shook his head. "Just telling you what was said. But it's all over. I got two texts about it last night."

Drake shifted his eyes out into the hallway. Muttered under his breath.

He and Ava had sat in the truck for a long time before and after meeting Lauer. There was nobody around.

Nobody had seen anything. If the story was out, it had to have come from Lauer.

In a quick movement he rotated back to his desk, grabbed his bag. Left everything else where it lay.

"I'm not going to make it to Local Government today," he said.

"Listen man, we didn't mean to get you riled up," Wyatt said.

"We're just letting you know what was said," Greg added.

Drake paused by the door. "No, I know. Let's just say a bad situation is now a little worse."

Two blank faces stared back at him.

"Can we help?" Wyatt asked.

"Thanks, but it's better you don't. At least not now."

Both faces shifted from blank to confused.

"I'll see you guys later," Drake said. Gave a small wave and went back up the rear stairwell.

He fished his cell-phone from his pocket and had it pressed to his face by the time he made it to the parking lot.

Ava picked up after the second ring.

"Hey, I was just about to head over. What's going on?" she asked. No formal greeting. Straight to business.

"You at home now?" Drake asked. His tone was even more serious than hers.

"Yeah?"

"Stay there, I'm on my way."

Ava started to reply but cut herself short. "What happened? Is everyone okay?"

"Everyone is fine," Drake said. "We're the ones knee deep in shit."

Drake could hear her breathing on the line. She said nothing.

"I'll explain on the way," Drake said.

Chapter Thirty-Two

It was by nothing but pure dumb luck that Notch spotted Drake coming out of the law school.

Two days of searching had turned up nothing of Beth. Or the girl he'd beaten the hell out of.

Nobody at all had been to their house. No activity to Beth's cell-phone.

Even a trip through the bunkhouse and scaring the hell out of every girl in sight had turned up nothing. Nobody knew anything.

It was like the both of them had just vanished.

That left Notch with one option. Try and determine who it was Beth met with on Thursday. It was slow and clumsy as hell, but it was all he had.

Worse for him, it meant he had to emerge from the shadows.

That morning, he'd gotten up with the sun and did his best to look presentable. Put on clean jeans. A fresh canvas shirt. Pulled his long, thin brown hair back into a ponytail. Hid his grey eyes behind mirrored sunglasses.

Even attempted to brush away some of the grime from his teeth.

He would damned sure never pass for a college student. At least this way he might not draw enough lingering stares to get him tossed off campus before he found what he was looking for.

Every thought in his head told him to take his binoculars with him. At the very least his camera with the zoom on it.

Staring at himself in the mirror though, he reasoned that showing up with either to a college campus might not be the image he was going for.

Instead, he opted for an old dog-eared Louis L'Amour. Chose a bench in the corner of the quad. Posted himself up at eight o'clock and kept a sharp lookout.

With the book open on his lap and his head tilted down, his eyes worked in constant sweeps across the grassy expanse. A couple of times he thought he saw his target, but both turned out to be false alarms.

If you've seen one inflated college student, you've seen them all.

It didn't take long for the hardback bench and the awkward position to start working on his lower back. Pretty soon thereafter his neck started to ache.

At the age of forty-two he could still put somebody in a world of pain. At the same time, all that exertion was starting to do the same to him.

Luckily, he didn't have to wait long.

Just after nine, the man he was looking for burst out of a building to his left. Made a direct line for the parking lot, walking fast and jabbering into a cell-phone.

Almost indistinguishable from a hundred other males on the quad at that time.

If not for the fervor with which he burst through the building doors, Notch would have missed him. Instead, he was on his feet and moving fast in the same direction.

His own truck was parked nearby, but he didn't have time to go for it. Had to hope to corner the guy somewhere out of sight. At the very least, get a look at what he's driving.

Notch left the book on the bench beside him. Bounded across the quad in long, stiff-legged strides.

A dozen heads turned to stare at him. Any hope of staying incognito was long gone.

Like he gave a shit.

Ahead of him the young man finished his phone call and walked to the rear of the parking lot. Climbed into a faded pickup truck and fired it up.

Notch made it halfway across the lot before the truck eased by. The driver never even glanced in his direction.

Notch spotted the license plate as the truck rumbled away. Repeated it to himself as he walked on through the lot and into the intramural fields across the street.

Yelena answered on the second ring. Just the sound of her voice set his nerves on end. "You've found her?"

"No," Notch said. "But I found him. Write this down."

He rattled off the license plate number. Told her it was from the state of Tennessee.

"I told you to find me a girl. You found me a license plate," Yelena said. Voice thick with disgust.

Notch matched the tone. "No, I found who she met with. Now you get on the phone with that fat ass Sheriff and get me a name and address."

Yelena remained silent.

Notch was not about to back down this time. They'd come to him. They needed his help a hell of a lot more than he needed theirs this time.

"Call me when you have it," he said. Hung up.

Walked back to his truck to wait for more information.

Chapter Thirty-Three

Ava's bottom just touched the front seat before the truck lurched forward. She let out a small yelp and slammed the door shut as they shot ahead to a stop light.

"What the hell's going on?" Ava asked.

Drake was still stewing. Both hands gripped the wheel. He was doing his best to swallow his anger.

He couldn't take it out on Ava. It wasn't her fault.

He damned sure couldn't let it out on who they were going to see. That would only make things worse.

"I was over in the clinic office this morning. Had a little chat," Drake said.

"Oh God. What did Lauer say?"

Drake shook his head. "Greg and Wyatt. Said the word on the street is we're both already up to our necks in it."

Ava made a face. Mulled the information.

"But that doesn't make any sense. How could..." She let her voice trail off. "Lauer."

"Lauer," Drake echoed. Bobbed his head. "Son of a bitch threw us under the bus."

Ava rested an elbow on the window sill. Pressed her hand to her forehead. "But that still doesn't add up. I mean, why would he do that?"

"You remember that list of people Beth rattled off to us the other day? This thing is big."

Ava rotated her head at the neck. Stared at him. "You really think he's involved?"

"She did say there was a lawyer involved to handle all the paperwork."

"Yeah, but he isn't the guy who was at the adoption hearing the other day," Ava said.

"No, but he's the guy that took us there," Drake countered.

Silence fell between them. There was just enough coincidence and circumstance to argue both sides.

Neither one liked it.

"Where are we going now?" Ava asked.

"DA's office," Drake said.

Ava grunted. They had discussed the option last night. Both agreed they wouldn't take it there unless something happened to force their hand.

Something had happened.

Drake maneuvered the truck through downtown. Came to a stop on the north end in front of an aging brick building. The title United States Attorney's Office - District of Montana was embossed on the side.

"We have an appointment?" Ava asked.

"Nope," Drake said. Exited the truck.

Ava did the same. "Do we care?"

"Not even a little bit," Drake said. Went for the front door. Held it open and motioned her inside.

"Careful," Ava whispered. "I might end up liking someone from Montana."

Drake continued to glower. "I am *not* from Montana."

Together they entered and unloaded their pockets for the bevy of Marshalls working the door. Passed through the metal detectors and on inside.

They paused just long enough to check the directory on the wall before going to the second floor.

The building was old by most city standards. Par for the course in Missoula. Lots of red brick and hardwood floors. Bright overhead lights.

Drake took the stairs two at a time. Had to wait at the top for Ava, who has having a much more difficult time in her skirt and blouse.

Still far overdressed.

They entered the DA's office at the same time to find things subdued, even for a Monday morning. A very tired looking secretary looked them both up and down as they approached. Pursed her lips.

"Can you help you kids?"

The word choice and tone was noted by both. Neither commented.

"Is the District Attorney in?" Drake asked.

"Do you have an appointment?" She could not have looked more bored. Even used a pencil to twirl her hair. Hair that should have been silver but was now an off-shade of orange.

"No ma'am."

"I'm sorry, he's in court all day."

Drake made a face, looked at the ground.

"How about one of the Assistant DA's?" Ava asked.

"We don't have Assistants here," the receptionist said. "We have Deputies."

Now both of them were making a face.

"Can we speak to one of them?" Drake asked.

"I don't know. Can you?"

Both of them exchanged a glance. Drake's said he would never hit a woman, but he wasn't above sending Ava over after her.

Ava's said she would let him.

Before either one of them could make good on their unspoken idea, a man stepped out from a back office. Tall, with short strawberry blonde hair pushed to the side. Moustache clipped tight. Cup of coffee in hand.

"Can I help you with something?" he asked.

Drake pushed out a sigh of relief. "Yeah, we were hoping to talk to a Deputy DA for a few minutes."

"What's this about?" the man asked.

"We would like to enlist the office's help," Ava said.

"And you are?"

The two exchanged another glance.

"For the time being, citizens," Drake said.

The man nodded. Checked his watch. "I have twelve minutes. That work?"

"We'll take it," Drake said.

The receptionist buzzed them past the front desk. They followed the man into his office, took up chairs across a cluttered desk from him.

The office was tiny. Just large enough to hold all three of them. Bookcases lined two walls. An L-shaped desk took the other two.

A handful of family photos and children's artwork filled in any free space.

The man introduced himself as Timothy Wise, Deputy District Attorney. He shook each of their hands in turn.

"So what brings you in today?" he asked.

Just as they had the day before, they rehashed the story. Unlike the day before, they went a little slower. Finished in five minutes flat.

When they were done, Wise sat and stared at his desk. Said nothing. Laced his fingers in front of him and frowned.

"You both say you're in law school, so I assume you know how this works?" he asked.

"Yes," Drake said. "Normally, not always, but normally, cases come to you from law enforcement."

"Right," Wise said. Lowered his chin to his chest. Continued to ponder. "Remind me again why you can't take this to the Sheriff?"

Drake opened his mouth, turned to look at Ava. Didn't have a good answer and knew it.

"We don't know," he managed. "All we were told was they were involved."

Wise's face went from pondering to troubled. "You also realize that this is an office full of elected and appointed officials?"

"We do," Drake said.

"And that there is an election in three months?"

Drake forced himself to stare Wise in the eye. "We do."

"And that if we go accusing the Sheriff of criminal activity, we're all going to be out of a job?"

"Wouldn't *he* be the one out of a job in this scenario?" Ava asked.

Wise raised his eyes. Looked at her.

"I tell you both what," he said. "Why don't you start in civil court? Get yourself a case together. Find some real evidence. Something to substantiate all these claims. If that works, then you bring this back here."

The air sucked out of the room.

Drake felt his jaw drop open. Tilted his head so he could see Ava in his periphery.

The look on her face was much the same.

"And then what?" Drake managed.

"Then you bring it back here, and I myself will handle the case," Wise said.

Drake continued to look at Ava. Pushed himself to his feet using the arms on his chair.

"Thank you," Drake said. "That's a very gracious offer." He made no effort to mask the sarcasm in his voice.

Beside him, Ava stood. They both shook Wise's hand and filed out past the receptionist, who looked smug and giggled.

Neither one said a word until they got back into the truck. Once inside, Ava smacked the dash repeatedly with the palm of her hand.

Drake squeezed the steering wheel until he saw little white lights dance before his eyes.

After several long minutes, he turned the truck on and pulled away. Cut a path across the north end of town.

"Where the hell we going now?" Ava spat. She pressed herself flat against the seat. Folded her arms over her chest and stared out the window.

"Back to The Hawthorne," Drake said.

"Why?"

"We need to talk to Beth. We have a civil case to file."

Chapter Thirty-Four

On the east end of Missoula sits Hellgate Canyon.

An imposing name if there ever was one.

The origin of it traces back almost a century and a half, to when Native Americans were the only inhabitants of the region. During that time, the Salish Indians used the pass to get to their bison hunting grounds to the east.

The narrow passages through the canyon made for an ideal ambush point from their rival Blackfeet tribe.

Some time later when French traders first passed into the Missoula Valley, they noticed the sheer volume of Salish remains in the canyon. The name was given by them and has stuck ever since.

On Monday morning, Sheriff Spore was sitting at the base of Hellgate Canyon when the call came in. Not a call over his radio, a call over his cell-phone.

His special cell-phone.

"Christ Almighty," he muttered. "The day just started."

He flipped open the phone and grunted a hello.

On the opposite end, Yelena read out the license plate number. Told him to run a trace and find it. Fast.

"You telling me how to do my job?" Sheriff Spore asked.

"Just find out who it belongs to. Then find him," Yelena spat.

Sheriff Spore fumed. Exhaled through his nose. "And then what?"

"And then call Notch."

The phone went dead a moment later.

Sheriff Spore flipped it shut. Tossed it onto the seat beside him. It landed with a dull thud and bounced into the hollow of his upturned hat.

He got on the horn and put out a BOLO - Be On The Lookout - for the license plate number. Changed the channel on his radio and called dispatch. Asked her to trace the plate.

Sheriff Spore sat and finished the last of his morning coffee. Screwed the cap back onto his thermos before firing up the engine and driving back into town.

Waited for somebody to get back to him.

Sharon Talbot, his dispatcher, struck first.

"Sheriff Spore, this is Dispatch. Over."

He snapped the radio up and held it to his lips. "Go ahead Sharon. What did you find out?"

"Truck is registered to a Drake Bell. Nashville, Tennessee."

Sheriff Spore grunted. The name was familiar. Too familiar.

"That wouldn't be the same...?" he asked.

"Very same," Sharon said. She was every bit the Griz football fan he was.

Great. By every account, Drake Bell had always been a model citizen in the community. Spoke at elementary schools. Took part in Big Brothers/Big Sisters.

Was also a damn fine ball player.

"What has he done?" Sharon asked.

"Um, nothing," Sheriff Spore said. "He's just wanted for questioning as a witness in a matter. His truck was spotted near the scene."

Sheriff Spore knew as he said it was thin. He hoped Sharon wouldn't press him on it.

She didn't.

"Okay," she said. "Anything else?"

"No ma'am. Thank you."

Sheriff Spore looped past campus and on through town.

For two years the arrangement had been perfect. Nobody got hurt. Everybody made money.

Those damn broads were getting greedy though. Early polls showed the mayor was faring only so well with voters. The odds of her receiving a second term were anything but certain.

They were looking to make as much money as they could while they still exerted some modicum of power.

Sheriff Spore snorted at the notion. In truth, the rest of the group combined could run them out of town based on pure power.

The problems with such an approach were multiple though. For one, they had their hooks into everybody. Deep. Bennett and his alcoholism. Schievers and Harken and their tryst. Tanner and his campaign financing.

Himself and his gambling.

The second problem was the money. Everybody in the group had gotten quite used to it. Most of the time they did little to nothing to earn it.

Now that they had to put forth a little effort, they couldn't very well just back out.

And of course, there was the problem of Notch.

On more than one occasion, Sheriff Spore had tried to use his resources to find out who the guy was. Where he came from. What his real name was.

Nothing.

In a technology based society, the man had achieved the impossible. He was truly off-the-grid.

"Sheriff, I've got a visual of the license plate in question," squawked a familiar voice through the radio.

Sheriff Spore had the mic back up in a flash. "Go ahead Anson."

"Parked on the curb on West Pine outside the US District Attorney's Office," Anson replied.

Sheriff Spore released the call button on the mic. Swore out loud.

They were already going to the prosecutor's. Worse yet, they were going to the federal prosecutor's.

"How would you like me to proceed?" Anson asked.

"Fall back," Sheriff Spore said. "I'm a few blocks away and closing now. I'll take it from here."

"Roger that," Anson said.

Two minutes later, Sheriff Spore pulled onto West Pine and eased to a stop. He slid into a diagonal parking place and killed the engine.

Watched the truck for several more minutes. Waited for Bell to walk outside and climb in, a young woman with him.

Biting back the bile that rose in his throat, he reached over and fished the cell-phone out of his hat. Did the last thing in the world he wanted to.

He called Notch.

Chapter Thirty-Five

Drake had tunnel vision.

He hunkered in low behind the steering wheel. Fumed. Tried to put together a plan of action moving forward.

Tried even harder to remember why he went to law school to begin with.

Across from him, Ava appeared to do the same. Her jaw was set, arms folded across her stomach. She said nothing.

It only took a few minutes to cross town to The Hawthorne. Traffic was light, most everybody in town at work or school. Drake pulled his truck in beside Rink's aging rig.

They climbed out and walked inside together. Both had classes and work they were missing at the law school. Neither one cared.

Together they entered the room to find Kade and Rink watching a movie on HBO. Beth reading a magazine in the armchair. Ella was nowhere to be seen, her bedroom door still shut.

Sage had left with them the night before. Ajax must have left some time in the morning.

"You're front tire is a little low," Rink said from the couch. Didn't take his eyes from the television.

A not-so-subtle way of letting them know he was doing his job. Had seen them coming a long way off.

"And you look damn good in a skirt," he added for Ava's benefit.

"We need to talk," Drake said. Ignored the comment from Rink. Aimed his gaze at Beth.

Beth lowered the magazine from in front of her. Revealed a pair of blue eyes that were twice their normal size. Her lower lip trembled.

"Something else has happened?"

"Yes, but not what you think," Ava said.

Kade muted the television. All three people stared back.

"District Attorney shot us down," Drake said. "Too afraid of election backlash. Didn't even hear us out."

"Do you think..." Beth asked.

"No," Drake said. "I don't think there was any foul play. Just a spineless bastard."

"Real chicken shit," Ava added.

"So what are you going doing to do?" Kade asked.

Drake and Ava exchanged a look. Sighed. They were still operating fast and loose here, fueled more by anger and disgust than sound logic.

Drake knew it. Could tell Ava knew it too.

"Civil court," Drake said. "It's not much, but it's a start."

"What's the difference?" Beth asked.

"In short? Nobody goes to jail, but you get paid," Ava said.

Beth's eyes somehow managed to get a little larger. "But I'm not looking to get paid. At least not beyond what I need to clear my debts. That's not what this was about."

"Again, it's a foot in the door," Drake said. "If we can uncover some damning evidence and find you a sympathetic jury..."

"Big money," Kade injected.

"Well, yeah," Drake said. "But more important, it will force the DA to take on the case."

"You really think that will work?" Beth asked.

"It will have to," Ava said.

Drake looked around the room. There was a bevy of empty food cartons. The bed in the second bedroom was unmade. Either the cleaning lady hadn't been by, or they had turned her away.

"Let's step into the bedroom," Drake said. "We need to talk."

"Don't mind us," Kade said. "I could use getting up and walking around for a few minutes."

"And this window offers the best view of the parking lot," Rink said. "Talk all you want. Just make sure she stays nearby."

Although he was tasked with looking after Beth, the comment was aimed at the other female in the room.

Drake pulled out chairs from the dinette set. Thrust one towards Ava, sank into one himself.

"Alright," Ava started. "The rules of civil court are a little different. Murder, kidnapping, etc. are all criminal offenses. Those have to be brought by the state. What we need is everything you can give us lower than that we can throw at them."

Drake held up a hand. Twisted it from side to side. "Before that even, why can't we go to the police with this?"

Beth's face fell blank.

"Everybody we talk to keeps starting there," he said. "It's a valid question."

"I already told you, they're involved," Beth said.

"How do you know?" Ava pressed. "Did you see them? Talk to them? What are they doing?"

"I don't know," Beth said. She raised her hands as if to exaggerate the point. "All I know is one day while I was working the kitchen, I heard the lady in charge talk about getting that 'damn lazy Sheriff' out to take care of something."

Drake and Ava exchanged glances.

"But you never saw him or anything?" Drake asked.

"Didn't have to," Beth said. "They weren't the kind to *ever* call the law. If they wanted him to take care of something, it meant he was on their side."

Drake muttered under his breath. Ava shook her head in disgust. Mumbled something derogatory about Montana.

For a moment Drake considered retorting about the corruption in Louisiana since Hurricane Katrina. Decided to let it go. Not the venue for a back and forth.

"So what about the contract?" Drake asked. "Do you have a copy of it?"

"No," Beth said. Shook his head. "The lawyer kept the only one."

"Who's the lawyer?" Ava asked.

"Something Bennett," Beth said. "The other girls said he did theirs as well."

"The guy from the hearing," Drake said.

Ava nodded.

That much made sense. It bore to reason that the Children's Services worker they'd seen was also involved.

A cannonball dropped down until it settled in Drake's stomach. Remained lodged there for several long seconds.

"You ever hear anything about a judge being involved?" he asked.

Three heads turned to stare at him. Rink kept his focus leveled on the parking lot outside.

"A judge?" Ava asked.

"I mean, the lawyer and the CS worker there were both involved. What if Judge Tanner was too?"

Ava's eyes slid closed. "Which would make filing a civil case completely moot."

"Yup," Drake agreed. Made a grim expression. Bobbed his head.

What little bit of color there was drained from Beth's face. "So what does that mean?"

Drake opened his mouth to try and reply. Never got the chance.

Rink sprung to his feet. Drew back the curtain to cover the few exposed inches of window. "Never mind that. Right now we have to move."

Four mouths dropped open at once.

"What's happened?" Drake asked.

"The Sheriff just pulled into the parking lot. They know we're here."

Chapter Thirty-Six

Rink took control. In a span of one minute he transitioned from a North Woods hillbilly to a drill sergeant barking orders.

Nobody made the slightest effort to contest him. He'd grown up fast as a single-parent Army brat. Knew what he was doing.

"Alright, here's how it's going to go," he said. "This is the first we've seen of them, so I'm guessing they followed you back here. If they know we're here, they know Beth is with us. Maybe Ella too.

"We're going to split into three groups. Ava, you're with Drake. You two go first, walk as natural as you can into the parking lot. Get in your truck, go on about your day. Play it as cool as possible.

"Kade, stay with Ella. Right now she's still asleep. Leave her that way. Maybe they don't know she's here. Maybe they don't care. We'll wait them out to see.

"Beth, you're with me. We'll wait a few minutes after they leave to see if the Sheriff follows. Then we'll bounce. Find a new place to hole up. Get everything you have together, but leave it all here with Kade. If somebody else is watching, we'll want it to look like we're just stepping out for a minute."

Every head in the room nodded. For a fleeting moment, Ava looked almost impressed.

It passed quickly.

"Wait," Drake said, weighed Rink's instructions. "Kade, you go with Beth."

Rink held up a hand in objection. "I thought you wanted me to watch her."

"I do," Drake said. "But right now nobody knows you're here. I'd like to keep it that way. Besides, if Kade takes her up to the rez..."

"Sheriff has no jurisdiction," Ava finished. Looked impressed for the second time in as many minutes.

Rink nodded. Checked the window again. Saw that the Sheriff had settled into the back of the parking lot. Remained seated in his cruiser.

Either he was watching them, or he was calling in reinforcements.

"Go now," Rink said. "Before he has backup here. Force him to make a choice. Keep a sharp eye out, call me if you see anything."

Drake nodded. Opened the door for Ava to leave.

Side by side they walked out into the bright midday light. Drake did his best to look natural. Ava was rigid.

"What's your favorite part of Montana so far?" Drake asked.

Ava's face twisted into a sour look. "What?"

"What's your favorite part of Montana so far?" Drake repeated.

"What the hell does that have to do with anything?" Ava snapped.

"Rink said to look natural. Right now you're uptight as hell, even for you."

Lightning quick, Ava reached out and smacked his shoulder. "What's that supposed to mean?"

Drake made a show of recoiling. Forced a laugh. "See, that's better. Much more you."

Ava's face went from incredulous to a half smile. Her shoulders slumped. She feigned another slap, but pulled back. "Damn it. You're right. And who says I like anything about Montana?"

Drake climbed into the truck, forced himself not to stare into the rearview mirror. Started it up and pulled away. "Oh come on, this has to be more exciting than anything going on in NOLA."

Ava gave him a surprised look. Said nothing.

"What?" Drake asked. Pulled back onto Broadway. Allowed himself a first glance into the mirror.

The Sheriff stayed parked in the rear of the lot.

"Just surprised to hear you refer to New Orleans as NOLA, though LSU is in Baton Rouge."

"I know that. We had a discussion about Death Valley on Saturday nights, remember?"

"We did," Ava said. Looked into her own rearview mirror. "Anything?"

"No, which is a bad thing."

"It is?" Ava asked. Eyes never left the mirror.

"I'd rather have them follow us than Beth, wouldn't you?"

Again Ava muttered under her breath. "Good point. Let's hope Rink is as good as you seem to think he is."

"He seemed pretty put together back there, wouldn't you say?"

Ava gave a begrudging shake of her head. "Yea, he did."

Drake pushed the truck across town. Continued to glance in his rearview mirror. Nothing unusual.

He took the long route back towards campus. Pushed through several residential neighborhoods. Watched the mirrors.

Nothing jumped out at all. Just the normal meandering interlopers of midday traffic.

"I think we're clear," he said.

"Good," Ava said. "Drop me off at my place so I can grab a few things. I'll meet you in the office later this afternoon and we can start drafting the court filing."

Drake grunted, nodded. Directed the truck back towards Ava's. "You still want to push forward on that?"

"We can go ahead and file," she said. "Doesn't mean we can't withdraw it if we decide to later."

Drake considered the option. "True. It will take a couple of weeks before we're scheduled to appear anyway."

"If not longer."

They slid to a stop in front of Ava's place. She climbed out, paused like there was something she wanted to add. Shook her head and closed the door.

Offered a small wave as he drove off.

Drake considered running home to check on Suzy Q. Remembered Ajax was there, decided to go straight to the law school instead.

Chapter Thirty-Seven

Sheriff Spore watched Drake Bell walk out of The Hawthorne, get into his truck and drive away. He wasn't quite as thick through the shoulders and chest as he used to be, but there was no denying it.

It was the same young man he'd spent many Saturday afternoons watching over the years.

He had no idea who the young woman was with him. Noticed she was attractive. Very well dressed.

Classy.

Sheriff Spore ran a hand over his hair. Shook his head.

He hated giving them over to Notch, but there wasn't really a choice. He knew somewhere inside was Beth, probably the other girl too.

There was no way in hell he was giving either one of them over to that sick bastard. At least Bell might have a fighting chance.

Nausea passed through him as he picked up the phone from the passenger seat. The first time he'd tried to call Notch, he'd lost the nerve. Hung up before the first ring.

This time, he had no other option.

Notch snapped it up mid-way through the first ring. "What have you got for me?"

"The owner of the truck is a guy from Tennessee named Drake Bell. He is on East Broadway headed back towards downtown."

Notch grunted. "Student?"

"Law school," Sheriff Spore corrected. "Used to play ball for the Griz. Stays out of the spotlight, but that still makes him something of a low-level celebrity in this town."

Notch paused, breathed heavily. "Meaning?"

"Meaning this isn't like the girls. People will notice if something happens to him."

Notch snorted. "Thanks for the tip."

Sheriff Spore said nothing. In front of him, two people emerged from the hotel. The young man also looked somewhat familiar.

A young woman in her final days of pregnancy.

Sheriff Spore felt his stomach drop again. She was without a doubt the girl they were looking for.

"Any sign of the girl?" Notch asked.

Sheriff watched the pair climb into a beat up truck and drive away.

"No," he lied. "We spotted Bell and a young lady having lunch at the Montana Club. No sign of anybody else."

Notch signed off without a word.

Sheriff Spore did the same. Dropped his cruiser into drive and exited the parking lot after the truck.

Chapter Thirty-Eight

The law school parking lot was much thinner than it had been that morning. The bulk of undergraduate classes meet on Monday, Wednesday, Friday or Tuesday, Thursday. A vast majority of those are scheduled on the hour during the morning.

It was just two o'clock in the afternoon, but the lot was over half empty.

Drake found a spot in the second row and pulled in facing the only entryway. He watched for almost ten full minutes, but couldn't see anybody tailing him.

Still, he couldn't quite shake the feeling he was being followed.

His cell-phone sat face down on the dash and he grabbed it, called Kade. It rang almost a half dozen times before Beth's voice answered.

She sounded out of breath.

"Hey," she said.

"Hey, where are you?" Drake asked. "Everything alright?"

"We are about ten miles outside of Missoula in Frenchtown. Heading north towards the rez."

Drake checked his watch. They'd only left the hotel a few minutes before. They must be flying to already be in Frenchtown.

"Everything alright?" he asked.

"The Sheriff has been on us since we left," Beth said. Small crack in her voice.

Drake felt the pulse start to pound in his temples. Forced his breathing to slow down. Processed what she'd just told him. He told her to let him know when they got somewhere for the night and signed off the call.

He swung out of the truck, grabbed his bag and went inside. Nodded a few hellos to people as he passed through. Ignored a handful of sideways glances.

The clinic office was empty when he arrived.

On his desk was a note from Wyatt that told him his absence that morning was commented on by their professor. A second note from Greg telling him when he was scheduled to man the clinic office downtown.

With a sigh he dropped down onto his chair and called his laptop to life. Quickly checked his email. On a lark, checked the GoGriz message boards to make sure nothing new had come in.

To his relief, nothing had. At this point, anything new would have come from the other side.

He attempted a few minutes of reading for the next day, but just as fast gave it up. He fished a dry erase marker from his desk and went to the white board on the wall.

Scribbled "Civil Claims" across the top of the board.

Beneath it he made a small bullet point and wrote out Contract. Underneath that he made several ticks marks.

Breach. Unconscionable terms. Unequal bargaining power.

Left a little space for any additional angles that came up later.

Dropped down and wrote Negligence. Beneath that he wrote Doctor, Lawyer, Child Services agent.

Went down a little further still. Spelled out Administrative. Judge. Child Services agent. Sheriff.

Drake backed away and folded his arms across his chest. Walked forward again and wrote DAMAGES in all block letters. Put a question mark after it and resumed his pose in front of the door.

He knew that Beth had said she only wanted to get what was owed her. To get back to even and start over somewhere else.

At the same time, she was now in a truck with Kade driving north onto the reservation. Hiding away from the very law that was sworn to protect her.

She was for damn sure owed more than just the pittance they had promised her.

Drake was so deep in thought, he didn't hear the sound of high heels on tile. Barely even noticed when Ava rounded the corner and stood in the doorway staring at him.

Not until she walked in and took up a post beside him did her presence register. Even then, neither one spoke as she matched his pose, staring at the board.

"I was thinking we could add child custody dispute to the list," Ava said. If she thought one way or another about the ideas he had already posted, she said nothing.

"Mhmm," Drake mumbled and drew an arrow to the side. Inserted it between Negligence and Administrative. "Thoughts on damages?"

Ava shook her head. "Not yet. I was debating that on the way over here too."

Drake nodded, flicked his gaze to the clock on the wall above the board. "You know, right now we only need a complaint.

We split these up, we can get that banged out in no time. Have it over to the courthouse this afternoon."

Ava's eyes bulged. She still kept them aimed at the white board. "You want to get this to the county clerk today?"

"Why not?" Drake said. "The sooner it's filed, the sooner it's on the docket."

Ava bit her lip. Considered the idea. "I guess. We can worry about drafting the actual briefs thereafter."

"And have you seen the size of that poor girl's stomach? She doesn't have much longer before she gives birth. Clock is ticking."

"Agreed."

"I'll take the opening, contracts, negligence?" Drake asked.

"That'll work," Ava agreed. "Any idea how what I should ask for in damages?"

Drake grimaced. "Any idea who I should name as the defendants?"

Ava smirked. "Touché."

Without another word, they both returned to their desks to begin drafting.

Chapter Thirty-Nine

Mayor Sloan fishtailed into the driveway of the compound. Threw gravel into the tall grass on either side. Never once slowed down as the tires spun over the loose ground.

Sneaking away on a Monday afternoon was no easy task. It had taken a feigned migraine to ditch her four-thirty appointment.

The combination of a migraine and menstrual cramps for her assistant to retract his offer to work from her home office.

Once away, she cut a direct path through town towards the Valley. Turned off her work cell-phone. Gripped the *other* one in her hand.

No matter how many times she checked the damn thing, not one word was coming through to her.

She had spent her life in public service. The last fifteen years in the higher rungs of city government. She was used to having information at her disposal the moment she wanted it.

Radio silence was enough to give her an actual migraine.

The SUV had not stopped moving when she jammed the gear shift into park and switched the ignition off. She left the keys where they were. Her purse rested on the passenger seat.

She wouldn't be here long.

Two additional cars sat out in front of the house as she strode across the condensed front lawn. Sheriff Spore's cruiser was self-explanatory.

The other she assumed belonged to Notch.

The front door was half open as she ascended the three stairs and pushed her way in. Stomped into the living room to find the two men and her sister already deep in conversation.

Make that deep in argument.

"What the hell do you mean you let her go?!" Yelena yelled at Sheriff Spore. Waved her hands about.

Across from her, the Sheriff was on his feet. His hands were shoved into his back pockets. Facial muscles twitched beneath his moustache. "I already told you, I can't go on the reservation like that. I don't have jurisdiction."

"Then why the hell didn't you send Notch after them?" Yelena snapped.

"You said he wanted the truck. I gave him the truck!" Sheriff Spore replied. He wasn't screaming at her, but he wasn't far from it.

"You know damn well we want the girl! The only reason we want the truck is because he *met* with the girl."

Mayor Sloan walked on into the room. All three turned to acknowledge her, some of the steam evaporating.

Sheriff Spore rocked back on his heels. Pushed out a heavy breath. "It was just through pure dumb luck that I even saw the girl. I stuck around in the parking lot a few minutes after the truck left so I wouldn't tip them off. Happened to spot them sneaking out the side door."

"Them?" Mayor Sloan asked. Walked over and stood beside her sister.

"The girl and another young man," Sheriff Spore. "Also a former Griz. I assume he's friends with Bell."

All three fell silent.

Behind them, Notch lowered himself onto the sofa. Propped a boot onto the corner of the coffee table.

"I'm sorry, are we boring you?" Yelena asked.

From the couch, Notch smirked. No attempt to hide how amusing he found everything taking place.

"I never said a word," Notch said.

"No, but you never have to," Mayor Sloan said.

And she meant it.

The bastard had a way of interacting that always set her skin to crawling. She and Yelena were paying the bills and calling the shots, but she never quite knew who was really in charge.

At least not where Notch was concerned.

Notch draped a wrist over his knee. Twisted his hand at the wrist. "Law Dog over here should have called me the second he saw her. He might have jurisdictional issues, but I sure as hell don't. This whole damn thing would be over by now."

Yelena sighed. "But since he didn't?"

"But since he didn't, I went ahead and did my job. Tailed the truck."

"And you found him?" Mayor Sloan asked.

Notch offered the same stained-tooth smile that made people cringe with unease. "Even better. I found out where his girlfriend lives."

Sheriff Spore's eyes slid closed. Stayed that way for several long seconds.

Mayor Sloan had no such hesitation.

"Find her. If she was with him, she knows where Beth is. If she doesn't, make her bring Bell to us."

The smile remained affixed to Notch's face. After several seconds, he raised a dirty finger to his brow. Offered a mock salute. "Yes ma'am."

He stood and left without another word.

Sheriff Spore remained in place and stared at the sisters. Both looked uncertain until the moment they heard Notch's truck start and descend the driveway.

Then they became self-righteous.

The second they did, Sheriff Spore shook his head and walked outside. Less than a minute later, he drove away as well.

Alone in the living room, they took up seats facing each other and settled into them. Mayor Sloan studied her sister, a near carbon copy of herself.

Hoped she didn't look as tired or haggard.

Knew that she probably did.

"Did I miss anything else important?" Mayor Sloan asked.

Yelena shook her head. Remained silent.

"When is she due again?" Mayor Sloan asked.

"Two weeks from tomorrow."

Mayor Sloan had no children of her own. Would never have children of her own. But she had been through this process enough to know a woman was most vulnerable during her last few weeks of pregnancy.

"We have to find her before she goes into labor."

Yelena said. "To hell with labor. The second we find her, we cut it out of her and toss the rest to Notch."

Mayor Sloan nodded her head. She'd been thinking the same thing for the last twenty hours. Was a little ashamed that such thoughts didn't seem to bother her.

Why would they though? A complete lack of humanity was what got them involved in this business to begin with.

Maria and Yelena Gulov were born to Russian immigrants almost a half century before in Seattle. Maria had been brought into the world less than two weeks after making the voyage from Saint Petersburg. Yelena just a couple of years later.

Just after Yelena was born, their mother took ill. Died before she reached three months old.

Young and alone, their father put the girls up for adoption two weeks later. He'd never wanted children or a permanent home. Wanted to travel the world, live the gypsy life he'd been brought up in.

The girls were his wife's idea. Once she was gone, any attachment he felt to them was gone as well.

For the next eighteen years, the girls bounced between foster homes and orphanages all over the Northwest.

Some were stable. Some were abusive.

None lasted long.

Both developed a thick distrust for people. A complete absence of compassion in any form.

In college at Washington State, Maria met a man from Missoula named Jeremiah Sloan. He came from old Montana mining money and harbored deep secrets.

Chief among them, his affinity for the same sex.

His family suspected as much and perceived it to be a major fault. Something they could not condone. Conditioned his inheritance on marriage to a woman.

A relationship of convenience was born.

Jeremiah used the arrangement to access the family's wealth and continue his dalliances into art, theater, dance.

The pre-nup she was forced to sign didn't offer Maria much wealth, but it offered something even more important. The family name. Something she used to launch a thus-far sparkling political career.

Some people in the state were already talking State Senator or Lieutenant Governor within the next few years.

Looming in the background the entire time was Yelena.

Backed by her sister's support and the Sloan name, Yelena was able to accomplish most anything she wanted. Unburdened by her sister's spot in front of the cameras, she quickly developed a reputation for ruthlessness.

After a lifetime of seeing themselves shuttled through the adoption system and the money they garnered at every stop, the sisters put the plan in motion.

Between Maria's post and Yelena's cunning, things came together fast.

The copious amounts of wanton greed that permeated the town hadn't hurt much either.

"Things seem to be falling apart," Mayor Sloan said.

Yelena shook her head. "One bad apple. Nothing more."

Mayor Sloan raised an eyebrow. Said nothing.

Yelena extended a hand towards the bunkhouse outside. "Take a walk through there. Most of those girls are happy to be here. This is the nicest place they've ever lived. They'll take what we offer and be glad to get it."

Mayor Sloan grunted in response. Her sister did have a point. They'd been going strong for over two years now with almost no problems.

"So we make an example of her and go on about our business," Yelena said. "By the time we're done, we'll have enough to either retire or get you to the Governor's Mansion."

Mayor Sloan snorted. Allowed the right side of her mouth to turn up in a half smile. "If we're going to do that, we're going to need to keep moving full speed ahead."

Yelena nodded in agreement.

"And if we're going to do *that,* we're going to need to do more than make an example of her. We're going to need to make an example out of everybody she's working with."

Yelena's eyes scanned the far wall as if searching for an answer. "You're right. We have to show these girls we can get them and anybody else we want to."

"Hmm," Mayor Sloan said. Nodded her head. Already the frustration she felt upon arrival was retreating.

Notch was going after the guy in the truck. They knew Beth was close by. It was only a matter of time before things fell back into place.

"We should get some more guys," Yelena said. The sound of her voice drew Mayor Sloan back into the room.

"You think? We've got Notch. That crazy son of a bitch hasn't needed any help before."

"Yeah, but we've never asked him to take on a whole group before either," Yelena countered.

Mayor Sloan considered it. Pushed herself up from her chair. Started towards the door.

"Make the call. Let's get this damn thing done."

Chapter Forty

A pleading.

Formal notification to the court system that something had occurred for which a party seeks intervention.

Step One in the legal process.

More style than substance, it is a very straight-forward listing of a party's grievances. One by one they are enumerated, along with a preliminary mention of what is sought in damages.

No actual arguments. No references to legal precedence. Not even a list of people that will serve as witnesses.

For the case of Beth Haggerty versus City and County of Missoula, the first draft took almost two hours to write. The first hour, Drake and Ava both typed furiously. Neither one said much.

The next half hour, Ava sent over what she had and Drake compiled it into an acceptable format.

The final half hour was spent debating the questions staring back at them. Who to name as the defendant and what to pray for in damages.

The kind of questions that should be taken to a mentor. One, for example, like a clinic advisor.

For obvious reasons, that option wasn't available.

After much debate, they decided to go after the City and County of Missoula. They had no idea what exact persons to name, but knew that the Sheriff, Child Services representative, and an attorney were involved. Maybe a doctor and judge as well.

Seemed as good a solution as any.

The damages took a little bit longer to hash out. Beth had been adamant that she only receive the money promised her.

Drake and Ava both agreed that wouldn't be enough. Not enough to cover the medical expenses she would now be responsible for or the physical and psychological trauma she was being subjected to.

Most important, it wouldn't put a dent in a criminal jury's mind. If they were using this as a stepping stone into federal court, they needed to aim high.

In the end, they decided to go with Beth's original request.

Times a hundred.

The last thing Drake typed into the pleading was the number two million dollars. He didn't even bother to reread it. Just hit save and printed.

Together he and Ava signed at the bottom. Left the law school at twenty before five.

The parking lot was nearly deserted as they emerged into the late day sun and climbed into Drake's truck. The busiest place on campus was now the intramural fields as they drove by, loaded with flag football and ultimate Frisbee players.

Neither one even bothered to look over at them.

Drake angled the truck through town towards the courthouse and parked in the quick-stop parking on the corner. Side by side they descended the short flight of stairs to the Clerk of Court's office.

There they found a short, plump woman in her mid-forties. Her thick hair was dyed a shade too dark and hung in tight curls around her head.

Even at eleven minutes before five, she already had her purse strap over one shoulder and keys in hand.

She frowned as they approached. "May I help you?"

Drake extended the pleading towards her. "We'd like to file this for the first available court date, please."

The woman sighed. Made an exaggerated show of looking at the clock on the wall. "Can it wait?"

"No," Ava said. Not even the slightest pause. No hint of sympathy in her voice.

The woman leveled a hard stare on them and held out her hand for the document.

Drake passed it over. Waited as the woman checked it to make sure everything was in order.

Cringed as her gaze passed over the named defendant. Smirked as it bulged at the sight of the amount prayed for.

After a minute of looking everything over, the woman pulled a heavy stamp out from her desk drawer. Slammed it down on the top of the form.

"Your hearing will be two weeks from today in front of Judge Tanner. Now if you'll excuse me, I've got my kid's soccer game to get to."

She left them standing in the middle of the clerk's office, muttering under her breath as she departed.

"That went well," Ava said.

Drake let the comment pass by and started for the door. "You hear who she assigned us to?"

"You caught that too, huh?"

Drake stepped out into the sun and stretched his hands high over his head. He had no idea where the day had gone, just that he was exhausted and famished.

At the same time, he also felt excited. It was the first time, even after the summer he'd had, that he felt like his being law school was having a positive impact on someone.

It would be a short lived feeling.

Chapter Forty-One

Unlike most people, Dr. Ben Schievers favorite day of the week was Monday.

Such a declaration might come as a shock to many people, but the reasoning was rather simple.

After his affair with Harken, his marriage went from ephemeral to non-existent. The infidelity his wife could overlook. His involvement in the ring she could not.

Hypocritical as it may be, she had no problem taking half the money he made from it to remain silent though.

The two had never wanted children, leaving him with a big empty house to go home to every night. He had no real hobbies to speak of. He didn't care for sports and hadn't turned on the television in months.

Weekends were the worst part of the week for him. He would tend to the yard. Wash his Lexus. Do what little bit of laundry he had.

Basically, just sit and watched the clock until the work week started again.

The odd part of it all was, once the week started he found himself thrust back into a ninety hour load that had him longing for the weekend.

An unending cycle of exhaustion and self-loathing.

At five o'clock the surgery ward receptionist poked in and wished him a good evening. She was cute and perky, the kind of person a younger version of himself would have spent endless hours fantasizing about. Maybe even trying to strike up a conversation with.

Now, he didn't even bother to look at her. Kept his face hidden behind a chart he was reading and waved one finger at her. Offered a perfunctory, "Night."

Dr. Schievers waited until her footfalls disappeared down the hallway and rose from his desk. He shut the door and locked it, then pulled his cell-phone from the desk drawer and hit speed dial number one.

Yelena's thin, nasal tone responded. "What?"

It always surprised Dr. Schievers how heinous Yelena came across on the phone. While no means a jewel in person, she was nowhere near as gruff as her automated persona let on.

Kind of like one of those hacks that will eviscerate someone from the safety of their laptop, then smile to their face.

"I was just calling to let you know, Beth missed her appointment today."

"No shit," Yelena snapped.

Dr. Schievers jaw dropped open. "Did something happen? Is there anything I should be aware of?"

"You know damned well what's happened. That's the reason you're calling."

Dr. Schievers mouth remained open. He stared blankly through his office window into the parking lot. Tried to think of something to say.

Nothing came to him.

"Is there anything else?" Yelena asked.

"I...I had no idea anything was wrong," Dr. Schievers said.

"Don't give me that," Yelena said. "You were here for the meeting yesterday."

Dr. Schievers eyes slid closed.

The meeting. He had assumed when they'd sent Notch to find the girl, he would find the girl. He had also assumed that they would at least keep her alive long enough to deliver the child.

Apparently he was wrong.

"So she's..." he asked.

"Still missing," Yelena said. Extreme annoyance in her voice.

Dr. Schievers eyes popped open. His eyebrows raised. Definitely not the response he was expecting.

"Okay," he mumbled. "Please keep me apprised if anything changes."

The line went dead without a response.

Dr. Schievers pulled the phone back away from his head and stared at it for several long seconds. Remained motionless until the disconnected line began to beep at him.

He turned the phone off and back on, placed another call.

It was answered on the third ring.

"Patricia Harken." Curt. Professional.

"Patty, it's Ben. We need to talk."

Chapter Forty-Two

Ava had Drake drop her off at her apartment.

It had been a long but promising day. She was exhausted, but a touch elated as well. No need to ruin that going back to the law school.

Whatever she had to do would still be there tomorrow.

She could tell by the expression on Drake's face that he felt the same way. They were nowhere near where they wanted to be, but they were pointed in the right direction.

It was the first time since landing in Missoula she'd felt even the slightest inkling of optimism.

She left Drake on the curb with a small wave and went inside. No awkward pep talks, no rah-rah speeches.

Just wasn't her style.

Instead she climbed out and walked straight up the side stairwell to her second floor apartment. Heard Drake drive away behind her, but didn't bother to turn and watch.

She unlocked both the knob and the deadbolt and went inside. Dropped her keys on the counter and took a long pull of water from the bottle she kept on the refrigerator door.

A habit she'd picked up from her mother a long time ago.

With one hand she reached back behind her neck and undid the string of pearls. Slid them from beneath her hair and laid them on the counter. Took another swig of water and headed towards the bedroom.

Already her mind was thinking about a quick run before dinner. Maybe some yoga.

She passed through the living room and into her bedroom. Made it two feet inside the door before something registered in her mind and she retreated three short steps.

Sitting on her couch was a man she had never seen before.

Judging by his weathered outfit and scruff appearance, there was a reason.

Ava felt a film of sweat immediately envelope her. Her breath drew tight in her chest. "Who the hell are you?"

The man said nothing. Continued to stare at her with his hollow gray eyes and vacant smile.

"How did you get in here?" Ava asked. She cast her eyes to her bag in the kitchen and thought of her cell-phone inside it.

The man noticed the glance. Made a soft tutting noise with his tongue. "I wouldn't do that if I were you Miss Zargoza."

Ava stood rooted in place. "How do you know my name? What do you want?"

The man raised his eyebrows as if bored. "Your name is of no matter to me, but I got it off a piece of mail anyway. I find having some personal information makes this whole experience a lot more real for you.

"*That* makes it a lot more fun for me."

"Makes what a lot more real? What do you want?"

Ava drew in deep breaths. Tried to force her heart rate to slow. To push aside her anxiety and think for a moment.

"So many questions. You'll make a great lawyer someday. Provided of course you survive to see someday."

Ava's heart began to beat even harder. The only person in Missoula she really knew had just driven away. There would be absolutely no reason for him to come back.

As far as she knew, her landlords downstairs didn't get home until late in the evening. Even if she screamed, the odds of anybody hearing it were remote.

The odds of anybody acting on it, even more so.

"Who are you?"

The man lowered his feet from her coffee table to the floor. "My name, like yours, doesn't matter. But since I do know yours, I'll extend you the same courtesy. You may call me Notch."

Ava tried hard to swallow down the lump in her throat. Fought to keep the fear back far enough so she could think.

What little bit of stuff she'd shipped up was still in boxes. The only things in the apartment were the sparse furnishings that came with the place.

Nothing that constituted a weapon.

Behind her was the bedroom. She could duck inside and slam the door, try to buy herself a few minutes. Maybe even enough time to make it to the window.

"Notch?" she asked. "Like in a headboard?"

The same vacant smile returned to the man's face. "You should be so lucky."

He didn't elaborate. He didn't have to.

This was a man that was used to killing. So much so that he'd even nicknamed himself after his craft.

There was little doubt he had no qualms about adding her to the tally.

"Why are you here? How did you get in?"

The man made a face. Lowered his gaze at her as if the question was foolish. "You think the Sheriff was the only one watching you guys this morning?"

Ava did her best to keep her face level. He was right. They'd been so caught up in watching for the Sheriff, they'd overlooked anybody that might be tailing them.

She inched her way back into the room. "How did you get in here?"

The man drew his feet up under him, pushed himself to a standing position. "Still with the questions. If I were you I'd be much more concerned with where I'm taking you than how long it took me to pick your lock."

Ava stopped moving backwards for a moment. Let the weight of his words sink in to her.

Took a deep breath.

In one movement she wheeled around and slammed the door shut behind her. Sprinted across the hardwood floor for the window.

She could hear his heavy footsteps coming. Literally feel the ground shake as he smashed through the door.

As fast as she could she unlatched the window and pulled upward on the wooden frame.

A recent coat of paint locked it in place.

Unable to think of anything else, she threw her head back and screamed as two fat teardrops rolled down her cheeks. In vain, she continued to press upward on the window sill.

The scream lasted less than a second before a heavy hand grabbed her by the nape of the neck and drove her head into the window frame.

Her vision, her entire world, went straight to black on contact.

Chapter Forty-Three

Drake was sitting on the couch when the call came in.

To his right was Suzy Q, her paws flat on his thigh, her chin between them. To his left were the remains of some chicken stir-fry he'd had for dinner.

The correlation there was unmistakable.

In the middle of the living room was Ajax, bouncing around as he acted out his newest creation for Drake to see. Some kind of first person warrior game for the Nintendo Wii.

As best Drake could tell, the player was the last remaining warrior in a medieval time faced with a zombie apocalypse. The idea was to fight his way from village to village and rally any remaining survivors using only basic weaponry and lead them to safety.

Talk about cramming as many clichés into one video game as possible.

To be fair, Ajax had taken the rather cheesy concept and made it quite entertaining. Ideas, after all, weren't his responsibility. Just the execution.

As the saying goes, that's why he made the big bucks.

Really, really big bucks.

It was fortunate Drake's phone was on vibrate. The volume on the game was so loud there's no way he would have heard it.

Instead he felt it pulsating beneath Q's chin, pulled it out and checked the caller ID. "Ajax, can you pause a second buddy?"

Ajax did as he was asked, turned and waited in the middle of the room. Stood panting from the exertion of the game.

"Hello?" Drake asked.

"Any word from the rez?" Rink asked.

"Kade called a little bit ago. They're at his grandmother's right now."

"Is it safe?"

"Fort Knox," Drake deadpanned. And he meant it. The Flathead Reservation was one of the most self-contained places he'd ever seen in his life.

They might not entirely accept the Keuhl family, but they damned sure didn't trust outsiders.

"Good," Rink said. "So listen, Ella is awake."

"She's awake? Is she okay? Do I need to call Sage?"

"No, no, she's fine," Rink said. "But we're both hungry, could use some fresh air."

The statement surprised Drake for a moment. He just as fast pulled back and realized it shouldn't.

They weren't prisoners. It was a more than reasonable request. "You guys going out to dinner? Do you need money?"

"No. We need to stretch our legs, not do something stupid that might get us seen. You mind if we come over? Maybe order in some Chinese?"

In the background, Drake could here Ella groan and mutter something intelligible.

"I mean some sandwiches," Rink added.

"Sounds like you two are getting along well."

"Just peachy. See now why I want to come by?"

Drake chuckled. "You know where we are. I'll have food waiting for you."

"Any chance you'll have that partner of yours there too?"

"Sorry man, not tonight," Drake said, smiling and shaking his head.

Both parties signed off as Drake rose and went into the kitchen. He called and ordered some subs for Rink and Ella, an order of wings for Ajax.

Some garlic bread for him and Q to share.

The food arrived at the same time as Rink and Ella. Despite their walking up to the front walk together, Ring pretended not to see the delivery man and let Drake handle all necessary transactions.

Once inside, conversation was at a minimum while the food was devoured. Ajax switched the game over for *Hawaii Five-O* and everyone watched as Steve McGarrett delivered canned lines in between shots of the gorgeous Oahu scenery.

Ajax waited until the episode was over to switch back to his game. He restarted in two player mode and gave a quick demo to Rink.

Within seconds they were battling like two modern day Knights of the Round Table.

Two mismatched, oddball Knights of the Round Table.

Drake watched with bemused detachment for a few moments before sliding over next to Ella. Between the volume of the game and the yelling from its combatants, he never would have heard her otherwise.

"Can we talk for a few minutes?"

Ella made a face that relayed she knew it was coming and was dreading it. She nodded her head in the affirmative anyway.

Drake motioned with his head towards an open door in the back of the living room.

Inside was the spare bedroom they'd demanded when choosing a place. If anybody asked it was for "out-of-town visitors," but the truth was it was so Sage or Kade could stay whenever they wanted.

And they often did.

The only difference between them was when Sage stayed, it was because it was late and she didn't feel like driving home. When Kade stayed, it was because he'd been out late and couldn't drive home.

Even still, the room was spotless. Smelled like vanilla candles.

Despite being two young males with a dog, Ajax and Drake were both meticulously clean. Some might even accuse them of being OCD about it.

Didn't seem to bother either one in the slightest.

Ella dropped down onto the pillow top mattress and laid back on the bed. She pressed a hand against her bloated stomach.

"I ate too much."

Drake smirked and settled into a rocking chair in the corner. "You've been out for basically three days now. Your body can't handle that much at once."

"It just tasted so damn good."

Drake couldn't help but laugh. She had stolen Beth's line without realizing it.

"Aside from food misery, how are you feeling?"

Ella raised the hand from her stomach to her temple. "Disoriented."

"That would be the sedative," Drake said.

"Explains why everything is so blurry," Ella said.

Drake leaned forward and rested his elbows on his knees. "I know you don't feel well, so I apologize in advance for asking, but what do you remember?"

Heavy sigh. "Not a lot. Rink filled me in on most of it. I remember coming home a couple of days ago like always. I pulled my car into the garage and came in through the side door.

"When I went inside, there was this guy sitting there."

"What guy?"

"I don't know. I'd never seen him before. Believe me, I'd remember if I had."

Drake paused a moment. Wondered if he should be writing this down. "What do you mean?"

"I mean, he was out there, even for Missoula. Looked like a cross between a mountain man and a Grateful Dead fan. Dressed in outdoor gear. Long hair. Vacant smile. Hollow eyes."

"Damn," Drake whispered.

"That's what I thought," Ella said. "Scared me so bad I couldn't move. What made it worse was he seemed to be enjoying it so much, he didn't even do anything. Just stood there and watched me."

"Did he say anything?"

"Not really. Told me to put my cell-phone on the table. Gave a couple of evasive answers to my mumbled questions. Nothing serious. Bastard just seemed to love seeing me squirm."

"Then what happened?"

Ella shrugged against the mattress. "He just kind of sat there. Waited until I tried to make a move back into the garage for my car.

"He was on me before I even reached the door."

Drake could hear cracks starting to ebb into her voice.

"Just a couple more questions, I promise," Drake said.

Ella sniffed. Nodded her head. They'd removed as many of her bandages as they could before coming over. Even still, she resembled a mummy lying there against the dark comforter on the bed.

"How did he know where to find you?"

Ella raised a hand to her cheek. Let a tear soak into the gauze. "I guess they followed Beth when she came over at some point. I don't know."

Drake nodded. He'd figured as much. If they were watching as much as Beth seemed to believe, they no doubt knew who Ella was.

Just from one lunch meeting they'd somehow spotted him and had the Sheriff tailing him around town.

"Did you leave the house unlocked? The front door was open when I went to check on you Saturday afternoon."

Ella sat up. What could be seen of her face was wet and blotchy. Heavy bags belied her eyes. Hair hung lank around her face.

She needed a bath, but it would have to wait until Sage could come by to reapply the bandages afterward.

"Never. I moved here from Denver, where we always lock everything. Habit."

Drake set his jaw. Nodded again. So whoever this was blended with the locals and knew what he was doing.

Neither thought was very comforting.

"Is there anything else? Anything at all?" Drake asked.

Ella shifted her eyes to the floor and pondered the question for several minutes.

"He said to tell Beth Notch said hi."

Chapter Forty-Four

The Double Front Café.

The very definition of a dive if there ever was one. Serving up fresh fried chicken and French fries to locals for decades.

Check that, serving up most anything fried for decades.

Pickles. Hush puppies. Corn fritters. Even macaroni and cheese. If a person has a hankering for good food with a side of angina, the Double Front has them covered.

Aside from the menu, the Double Front offers a second luxury to all patrons.

Privacy.

Long held as a local treasure, the place is spoken of in hushed whispers. Half out of respect, half out of keeping it a secret, the place is held very close to the chest by locals.

Many appreciate that there is never a line. Others find it provides the perfect place for quasi-clandestine meetings like the one taking place tonight.

Judge Tanner was the last one of the group to arrive. He made no attempt to hide his contempt at the entire affair and waved off the waitress as she waddled over to take his order.

"What the hell are we doing here?" he asked.

The dining room was empty. This time of evening, most of the guests were in the basement shooting pool or flipping cards.

Still, he kept his voice down.

The rest of the group was arranged around a sweeping corner booth that more than housed all five of them.

How comfortable it was depended on their thoughts towards cheap vinyl.

"We're just a bunch of friends meeting after work," Dr. Schievers said. He motioned towards the baskets of fried food in the center of the table and the random assortment of water, coffee, beer between them.

None of the food or drink looked like it had been touched.

Judge Tanner rolled his eyes and looked over the rest of the group. "Why are we really here?"

"Doc's losing his nerve," Bennett said a little louder than necessary. Very matter-of-fact in his tone.

Sheriff Spore held a hand out to Bennett. "Hey now, let's not go making snap judgments. Let the man speak."

Dr. Schievers looked at the Sheriff and nodded. Tried to work down the lump in his throat. "You all remember the meeting yesterday, right?"

Judge Tanner sighed. "We were there."

"Do you know they still haven't found her yet?"

Judge Tanner opened his mouth. Paused. Closed it. "Still?"

Dr. Schievers shook his head and glanced back to the Sheriff.

"No," Sheriff Spore said. "I got a line on her today, but she fled onto the reservation."

"So?" Bennett said.

Sheriff Spore made a face. "For a lawyer, you're not very damn smart are you?"

Bennett leveled a glare back at him. "I know all about jurisdictional issues. But this isn't the sort of thing that will ever make it into a court of law, is it?"

"The baby is," Dr. Schievers retorted.

Bennett declined further comment. Sat and fumed at them both.

Judge Tanner leaned back and folded his arms across his chest. "Again I ask, why are we here?"

Four sets of eyes stared at Dr. Schievers. His cheeks took on a pink tinge beneath the harsh overhead lighting.

"They're going to kill her you know."

The group remained silent for a moment.

"I talked to Yelena this afternoon. She all but told me they're going to cut the kid out and feed the girl to Notch."

Bennett and Judge Tanner both exchanged a look. A bit of the hostility fled from their faces.

Dr. Schievers lowered his eyes to the table and dropped his voice another decibel. "We all remember what happened last week. I can never, ever, be a part of something like that again."

Beside him, Harken's eyes slid shut. A tear rolled down her face.

"So that's why you called us here?" Bennett asked. "Try to stage some sort of coup?"

"Because in case you haven't noticed, this little arrangement has been damn good for all of us," Judge Tanner added.

"I'm not saying it hasn't," Dr. Schievers said. "And I know we've all had our transgressions that led to us being here."

Most of the group shifted in their seats. It was common knowledge that everyone had at least one red flag that had got them noticed.

Quite another to acknowledge it out loud.

"And for the last few years, we've all played our part. All of us. Nobody any more guilty than the others. But what happened last week..."

Judge Tanner and Bennett again exchanged a glance.

Dr. Schievers saw it. Looked at each of them, then the rest of the table in turn. "Look, I'm a doctor. A long time ago I took an oath to help people. For two years I've been able to wake up in the morning by telling myself that at the end of the day, we were helping these children."

"And you think the rest of us are blood sucking leeches that only care about money?" Bennett challenged.

"I didn't say that," Dr. Schievers said. "But look around the table. We have a judge. A lawyer. A Sheriff. You guys are used to seeing the worst the world was to offer.

"I won't speak for Patty, but I for one am not. This isn't what I signed up for."

Silence fell over the table.

Several uneasy glances were exchanged. There was less hostility than even a few minutes before, but still an uneasy tension remained in the air.

"So what do you want to do?" Judge Tanner said.

"I don't know," Dr. Schievers replied.

"You all know at this point, this has to be a group decision, right?" Judge Tanner said. "We're way too deep into this for anyone to walk."

"Let's just slow down a minute," Sheriff Spore said. "I don't think anybody's said anything about a decision being made. We haven't even talked about all the options yet."

Judge Tanner shook his head and kept his eyes locked on the untouched ice water in front of Dr. Schievers. "There are no options. Either we're in, or we're out."

Bennett leaned in and smacked his palm on the table. "Listen to you people, all sitting here discussing this as if there's a choice to be made. You realize what they'll do if we try to go anywhere?

"They'll send that sick bastard Notch after us. Have us all replaced by this time next week."

The air sucked away from the table once more. Just the mention of Notch's name had every one on edge.

"Just think, next time it could be one of us strung up in that barn."

Bennett leaned back in his seat. Let the words penetrate the group.

They had the intended effect.

"Is everybody in agreement that we aren't going anywhere?" Judge Tanner asked. Any edge of hostility from earlier was gone. Now, he just seemed tired.

Bennett and Harken both nodded.

"I'm not happy about it, but he's right," Sheriff Spore said.

"Same here," Dr. Schievers whispered. "The thought of looking over my shoulder for that sick son of a bitch..."

The table nodded in agreement.

Let that scenario play out in their heads.

Nodded some more.

Chapter Forty-Five

Many people pay good money to visit Western Montana.

To rise with the sun. To watch as it first appears out of the east and splashes down through the Bitterroot Valley.

Mayor Sloan was not one of those people.

She barely noticed the orange glow that illuminated the horizon. Didn't even look at the streaks of purple that extended through the sky above her.

Instead, her eyes followed the darkened pavement in front of her. Focused atop the bright orbs her headlights threw out into the dawn.

Her hands squeezed the steering wheel so hard her knuckles went white beneath her skin.

Coming out for an early morning meeting might be easier than an afternoon one, but she was still ready for the entire situation to be over.

The sooner they found the girl, removed their property and buried her ass, the better.

The high beams on her SUV bathed the front of the house in light as she pulled up. The second she shut off the car, semi-darkness enveloped everything once more.

The only illumination was nature's pyrotechnics going on above.

The only sound a crescendo from the river nearby.

Mayor Sloan didn't bother to knock, just pushed her way through the front door and into the living room.

Stopped short as a half-dozen stares leveled on her.

Make that, leveled *down* on her.

Mayor Sloan drew in a sharp breath of air. Recovered just as fast and repositioned the customary scowl across her face.

In front of her were six guys. None older than early twenties, some not even looking legal.

Every one weighed at least two hundred and fifty pounds.

Down the hallway, Yelena emerged carrying a coffee mug in one hand. She tilted her head back to motion for her sister to join her.

Mayor Sloan left the young men all standing in the living room. Nobody said a word on either side.

Her squared heel shoes made a loud knocking sound against the hardwood floors as she descended the hallway and stepped into the kitchen. She wrapped her hands around a mug of coffee on the counter she assumed was hers.

"That was fast," she said. No preamble.

"Like you said, let's get this thing over with," Yelena said. Took a slurp of coffee, as casual as if they were discussing the weather.

"Hmm," Mayor Sloan said and took a drink as well. Pumpkin spice, just as she liked. "Who are they?"

"Bunch of kids from Butte," Yelena said. "I called in a favor."

Mayor Sloan's eyes flicked to her sister. "Who do we know that owed us a favor in Butte?"

"*We* don't know anybody," Yelena said. "But there were plenty of people all too happy when you unseated a certain mayoral incumbent. I called upon one of them."

Mayor Sloan frowned. It was no secret that her predecessor had made a lot of enemies in his four years in office. His 'Going Green' initiatives had put the squeeze on a lot of businesses in the area.

Many of them had been her biggest backers in the last election.

Still, she hated actually calling on them. Especially in a manner that might draw attention to what they were doing.

"What story did you give them?"

"Told them you were going to be doing some outreach events in the coming weeks and we were looking to put on some full-time security staff for awhile."

"And they bought it?"

"No questions asked."

Mayor Sloan grunted and took another pull on the coffee. Waited as the warm liquid traveled through her body. "Kind of ironic, seeing as how most of them don't even look old enough to vote."

Yelena snorted. "That's just because we're getting old. They're plenty old enough. Besides, we don't need them to vote."

"True," Mayor Sloan conceded. "What have you told them so far?"

"Nothing. Was waiting on you to get here."

Mayor Sloan grunted again. Finished the last of her coffee and checked her watch. "I have a breakfast meeting in forty minutes. Let's do this."

Yelena tossed back the remainder of her drink and followed her sister down the hall.

The low sound of chatter in the living room died away as they entered. All six young men turned and looked at them.

Mayor Sloan and Yelena stood and stared back.

Of the six, three carried their bulk well. They were broad shouldered and thick through the hips. Quite capable looking.

The other three were a little sloppy. More window dressing than anything.

Still, all six were quite large. It would instill the image they were going for.

"Thank you all for being here on such short notice," Yelena said. "And for being on time this morning. Let that be a lesson too. If you're late, you're fired. Simple as that."

Nobody said anything.

"You were told you'll be working security for me," Mayor Sloan said, "which is true to a degree. You'll be security and you'll be working for me."

"All you need to know is, be where we tell you when we tell you," Yelena said. "Could be the easiest money you've ever made."

Everyone remained still, stayed silent.

Yelena tossed the top of her head towards the far wall. "You all should have seen the bunkhouses when you pulled in. You'll be in the second one.

"Go get yourselves settled in, and be quiet about it. If you guys wake up the girls, there'll be hell to pay."

A few of the young men's faces twisted up a bit.

They were wise not to voice any questions.

Mayor Sloan and Yelena stood and watched as they all filed out of the house. They kept their arms folded across their chests and said nothing until the room was empty.

"You see the ruddy cheeks on some of those boys?" Mayor Sloan asked.

"Let's hope all they have to do is stand around," Yelena said. "Remember, we have Notch to do the real work."

Notch.

Just hearing the name made Mayor Sloan feel a little better knowing she had him to clean things up if it got any messier.

"Yeah we do," Mayor Sloan said and strode from the room out towards her car.

She was back on the highway headed for breakfast three minutes later.

Chapter Forty-Six

Land Use Planning.

The study of public policy so as to regulate all government lands in an efficient and ethical manner.

No less than three contradictions in the one line course description. Still, it was a two credit class that met once a week. Pretty much the only two requirements Drake had when scheduling in the spring.

If it wasn't already too late to take something else, he would.

Tucked away in the far corner, Drake did his best to make it through the class. Conducted an email conversation with Greg and Wyatt on either side of him. Checked his fantasy football team. Read the Sports Guy on ESPN.

Minutes crawled by.

When it ended he begged off a mid-afternoon trip to the Food Zoo with the two of them and instead opted for a quick run up Mount Sentinel.

He figured he could shower at the rec center and be back in the clinic office in under an hour. He hadn't yet seen Ava for the day, but needed to talk to her.

Just because the pleading was filed meant nothing. They now had a brief to draft. The real heavy lifting of the operation.

The afternoon sun felt warm on his face as he stepped out through the front door of the school, Greg to his left, Wyatt to his right.

A gaggle of co-eds walked by, talking in squeals. Handful of blondes. Couple of brunettes and redheads thrown in for good measure. All young and wearing tank-tops.

One of the few joys of still being on a college campus at the age of twenty-four.

"You see that one smile at me?" Greg asked as the girls slid by. "In the purple shirt?"

"Um, I don't think she was smiling at you," Wyatt said and slapped his friend on the back. Nudged him on towards the parking lot with his fist.

"Oh, sure," Greg said. "They're always looking at the football star. The one who won't do a damn thing about it."

Drake smiled and shook his head. "Can't you all just enjoy the scenery while it's here? Need I remind you what happens in just a few short weeks?"

Wyatt grumbled. "Ugh, sweater season."

"Nine months of it," Drake added.

This time both Greg and Wyatt shuddered. A practiced two man dance that made Drake laugh out loud.

He turned and went for the parking lot without another word. Stopped by his truck and exchanged his land use planning books for a gym bag. Ducked into the rec center at the opposite end of the parking lot and changed in the locker room.

Ten minutes after fleeing a dungeon-like classroom, he was circling the back end of campus.

Gym-shorts swinging along his thighs. T-shirt bouncing over his shoulders. Running shoes slapping the pavement beneath him.

Drake opted against the front face of the mountain. Away from the famous M Trail with its switchbacks and scads of hiking tourists.

Went around back instead. Took an unmarked path and ran through the trees.

The backside was deserted as he wound his way up. The only sounds were his feet beating against the soft dirt of the trail and his own breathing.

The run to the top took a little over twenty minutes to finish, all of it fast and moving hard. By the time he reached the summit his heart was pounding in his ears. Sweat drenched his body.

Drake slowed to a walk on the peak of the mountain. Peeled his shirt off over his head. Let the Hellgate Canyon breeze blow across him.

From fifteen hundred feet above town, the world looked pristine.

Below him extended the Missoula River Valley for miles in all directions, every possible shade of green sewn together in a mottled weave. The Clark Fork and Blackfoot Rivers and their tributaries cut meandering stripes through it like spokes on a wheel.

Below him was the University of Montana campus. Washington-Grizzly Stadium. Missoula, laid out in perfect grid format.

Drake considered starting his way back down but opted to linger a little longer.

In a just a few weeks everything would be awash in gold and red. For the moment, it resembled Ireland in the spring.

Drake ran his t-shirt over his face once more. Tucked it into the waist band of his shorts and took a few steps down the front side of the mountain when his phone rang.

Usually, even bringing it would be a major faux pas. The fact that right now there were two girls under his indirect care made him do it anyway.

It took several steps for Drake to slow down. The sharp downhill made it hard to stop his momentum.

"This better be important," he muttered and pulled the phone from the zipper pocket along his waist line. Coughed from the cloud of dust he'd just kicked up.

Checked the caller ID.

Ava.

Drake pressed a finger to his left ear. Lifted the phone with his right. "Hey there. Taking the day off are you?"

The fierce mountaintop breeze was his only response.

"Hold on, I can't hear you," Drake said and stepped off the trail. He lowered himself to the ground and leaned his head forward between his knees.

"Alright, that's better. What's up?"

"I said, I haven't taken the day off. Been quite busy in fact."

Drake's head shot up. His breath caught in his chest. The voice was damned sure not Ava's.

"Who is this?" Drake asked.

"Who I am is of no consequence," the voice said. It was a man's voice. Low and graveled, a streak of something that sounded almost amused. "What you should be asking is what I want."

"Why are you calling me? And why do you have Ava's phone?"

Drake feared he already knew the answer to both questions. For some reason, deep down, he needed to be sure. He needed to hear the words.

"Again, you should be asking me what I want."

Drake's eyes slid closed. He tried to swallow but his parched throat wouldn't allow it. "What do you want?"

"Very good," the voice said. "I want to make a trade. The girl for the girl."

Drake's mind swam. He had no idea what to do next.

"What girl?"

The man on the other end tutted at him. "Don't play stupid with me Mr. Bell. I happen to know you are quite intelligent and know who I'm referring to."

Drake felt his stomach drop another few inches. Whoever was calling knew who he was. Knew he had Beth.

Had Ava.

Drake only had one card left to play. He prayed it wouldn't be her undoing.

"Yeah, I happen to know a lot about you too, *Notch.*"

The man on the other end paused for a few moments.

Drake held his breath. Hoped he hadn't just made a fatal blunder.

"Very impressive," the man said. "The girl must have remembered more from our little encounter than I gave her credit for."

Drake let out a small puff of air, relieved that he hadn't just condemned Ava.

It was soon replaced by unadulterated hatred. Anger at a man who enjoyed destroying females.

"What do you want?" Drake asked again, an involuntary edge to his voice.

"I appear to have hit a nerve," the man said. "Good. It's about time I got your attention."

He paused.

"Tell you what. I'm going to give you awhile to think things over. To sit and contemplate all the fun I'm having with your little friend here."

Drake gripped the phone so tight he could hear the plastic cracking. Didn't trust himself to say a word.

"I'll call you with further instructions when the time is right. Until then, go get the girl from the reservation. And keep your ass away from the cops.

"We'll be watching."

The phone went dead without another sound.

Drake sat still for a full minute and tried to wrap his mind what had just taken place.

A middle-aged couple walked past him up the trail. Both looked like they'd been through hell. Waved and said hello anyway.

It was all Drake could do to register their presence, let alone respond.

Once the breath returned to his chest, he started to run through what he knew.

The man was a psychopath that went by the name Notch. He had kidnapped and decimated Ella without remorse. He had entered her house and Ava's apartment undetected. He knew all about Drake and where they were keeping Beth.

He had Ava's cell-phone.

Drake dropped his attention back to his own phone. Hit speed-dial two. Waited for it to connect.

"Talk to me," Ajax responded.

"I need a favor."

"Where the hell are you? A wind tunnel?"

Drake ignored the question. "I need a favor."

Ajax paused. His voice went from normal to serious. "What's up?"

"Can you trace a cell-phone? Access its GPS?"

"Easily," Ajax said.

Drake could hear him moving through their place. Hear the sound of plastic wheels on hardwood as Ajax slid in front of his computer.

"Who am I looking up?"

"Ava," Drake said and read off her number.

Ajax fell silent for a moment. The clatter of him working a keyboard poured through the phone.

"Nothing, man. She must have it turned off. What's going on?"

"He has her," Drake said through gritted teeth.

He hated the taste of the words in his mouth. The sound of them in his ears.

"Oh shit..."

"Yeah," Drake muttered.

In the background, he heard Ajax relay the information. A thought occurred to him. "Who's there with you?"

"Sage just left for work. Rink and Ella were on their way back to the hotel."

Drake stood. "Ask Rink if he can meet me at the base of Mount Sentinel in ten minutes."

Ajax relayed the request. Paused. "He's on his way."

"Thanks."

Drake kept his phone in one hand, his shirt in the other. In long strides, he took off down the front of the mountain as fast as his legs would allow.

Chapter Forty-Seven

For the first time ever, Drake was *that guy.*

The guy that's a complete, unapologetic jackass in a public setting.

The guy that other people look at with faces mixed in disgust and disbelief.

The top half of the descent was almost vertical. Drake's feet barely touched the ground as he hurtled forward. Sweat rolled from his body. Dust swirled around him.

He couldn't have cared less.

Midway down, he entered onto the M Trail. Large handfuls of families dotted the trail. Many ranged in conditioning from athlete to couch potato.

Drake blew past them all. Yelled for people to move out of the way. Disregarded the switchbacks and went straight down the mountainside when the crowd got too thick.

Ignored the stares and not-so-silent comments behind him.

Despite the length of the trail, he made it down in twelve minutes. He could see Rink's truck tearing past the stadium as he descended and kept running across the parking lot to meet up with him.

The truck slowed as Drake tore open the passenger side door and slid inside.

"The son of a bitch has her?" Rink asked.

Drake was breathing too hard to respond. He nodded his head. Used his shirt to wipe the sweat and dust from his burning eyes.

His entire body was caked with both. Some of it smeared onto the door to his right. Some smeared across Ella's sweatshirt to his left.

"Where we going?" Rink asked.

Drake drew in two more gulps of air. "Downtown. Pine Street."

Rink angled his truck in that direction.

Drake continued to draw in deep breaths and rolled down the window in hopes of air drying a bit. He wiped the dust from his face and forearms with some McDonald's napkins from the floor.

"Where to now?" Rink asked.

Drake pointed out the District Attorney's office a block down. "There's no chance in hell this will work, but I've got to try anyway."

"Do we have time for all that?" Rink asked as he pulled the truck into the same diagonal parking spot Drake had used a few days before. He jammed the gear shift into park, but left the engine running.

"Probably not," Drake said and cracked open the door. "But they have more resources than we do. Right now we have to think about what's best for Ava."

Rink nodded, said nothing.

Drake pulled his shirt on over his head. The gray cotton clung to his sweaty skin.

He slammed the truck door shut and ran inside. The U.S. Marshalls eyed him as he handed over his cell-phone and stepped through the metal detector.

Twice reminded him the building closed in ten minutes.

Drake nodded, assured them he wouldn't need that long. Apologized for his appearance.

His blood still boiled, but he did his best to keep it under wraps. The last thing he needed was to raise the ire of a group of armed federal officers.

If all went to plan, some of them might even be following him from the building in a few minutes.

Drake dashed up the stairs two and three at a time, didn't bother even speaking to the same orange-haired receptionist sitting at the front desk. Instead, he slid over the desk *Dukes of Hazzard* style and landed softly on the opposite side.

He was past her before she even noticed enough to object.

In determined strides he went straight into Timothy Wise's office and wrapped harder than he intended to on the door with the back of his hand.

A moment later the receptionist appeared at his side.

"Young man, I don't know who you think you are or where you think this..."

"Shut up," Drake said.

She pulled back, aghast.

"I'm sorry," Drake said, "but this is important. I don't have time for your secret password games today."

Drake turned his attention back to the desk. Behind it, Wise looked quite annoyed. Not yet hostile, but getting there fast.

Drake knew he was on thin ice, especially coming in to ask for a favor. He only hoped the enormity of the situation would earn him a pass on his behavior.

"Ava's in trouble," he blurted out.

Ire turned to confusion. Wise made a face, tilted his head. "Excuse me?"

"Ava, the girl that was with me on Monday, she's in trouble."

Wise frowned. Leaned back and folded his arms across his stomach. "Is this about that same case you brought in here a few days ago?"

"Yes," Drake said. "Only it's gotten worse. Now Ava's been abducted."

"Abducted?" Wise said. "And what makes you say that?"

"Because they called me from her cell phone, told me as much," Drake said.

"They called from *her* cell phone?"

"Yes."

"Did you get a name or location?"

Already Drake could see where this was going and felt the venom begin to well up within him again. With a quick breath, he tried to remove what of it he could from his voice.

"All I know is the guy goes by the name Notch. He wasn't nice enough to tell me where he holds his kidnap victims."

Wise's frown grew deeper. "And tell me again why you can't go to the police?"

"Because they're involved!" Drake spat. "You think I'd be wasting time with you condescending pricks unless I had to? Local police won't help any. I need federal. That's you."

Drake sensed movement by his shoulder. Turned to see the receptionist looking past him into the office.

"Timothy, I've notified the marshals. They'll be up in just a minute."

Wise nodded. The receptionist disappeared.

"Look," Drake said, "we did what you suggested. Filed a civil claim. But this is bigger than that right now. This isn't about court hearings or procedure.

"They're going to kill her if we don't do something."

Behind him, he could hear the door to the office open. Two men's voices, followed by a stream of babble from the receptionist.

His time was up and he knew it.

Out of frustration, he tossed his hands in the air. "Fine, sit here on your ass and do nothing.

"But I'll tell you this, if anything happens to that girl, I'll make sure the whole damn state knows your role in it. How's that going to look for the voters this November?"

"Come on son, it's time for you to go," the closest marshal said. He had one hand out towards Drake, motioning with his hand.

Behind him stood a second marshal, hand at his hip.

Drake couldn't see the man's weapon, but he knew it was there.

Despite the torrent of words he still had for Wise, he said nothing. Nodded and left through the front door of the building.

The marshals followed him out onto the sidewalk. Watched as he climbed into the truck and Rink pulled away.

"I take it that didn't go well?" Rink asked.

"Chicken shit bastards," Drake mumbled, turned his head to Ella. "Apologies for the language."

Ella waved a hand. Said nothing.

"Where to now?" Rink asked.

Drake remained silent a moment and contemplated his options.

There were decidedly few of them. None were very appealing.

"I need another favor," Drake said.

"Name it."

"It might get messy," Drake said.

He didn't bother to elaborate further. Part of didn't want to spell it out in front of Ella. Part didn't want to stifle whatever Rink might have up his sleeve for such a situation.

"Name it," Rink replied.

Not the slightest hint of hesitation in his voice.

Chapter Forty-Eight

Drake pointed Rink back in the direction they'd just came and gave him an address a few block from the law school.

Rink's eyes bulged. "He's keeping her on campus? Why the hell didn't we start there?"

"No," Drake said. "I have no idea where he's keeping her, but I think I know somebody that does. That's where you might come in."

Between them, Ella remained silent. If she had any objections to what might take place, she didn't raise them.

Drake directed Rink when to turn and told him where to park. He climbed out and waited as Rink selected a wrench with a two-inch head from the bed of his truck.

Together they strode for the front door. Ella remained behind in the truck.

"I'm going to go up to the front door," Drake said. "I'm going to ask him once and only once. After that, do your thing."

"I got your back," Rink said. He remained behind on the sidewalk.

Drake walked up the three short steps to the front door and ignored the door bell. Instead, he opted to pound against the polished oak with the ball of his fist.

After the last few minutes, he had to admit it felt good to hit something.

It took three aggressive bursts of knocking before the door finally opened.

Behind it stood a very angry Lauer.

If Lauer noticed how pissed Drake was, he ignored it. Instead, the tiny man burst forth from the door frame as if he might hit him, even shook a finger in his direction.

"I thought I told you to *never* come here again!" he bellowed. He kept coming forward, brandishing the finger in front of him.

His anger quickly receded as he realized Drake was not retreating. He even had to pull up short just to keep from running chest-first into him.

Drake stood with his fists clenched by his side and glowered down at his Professor. He shifted his body to the side.

"Just so were clear, that man standing behind me is my friend. That wrench in his hand is very, very real. You might be a big time attorney, but right now neither one of us gives a damn.

"So be very careful about the next words out of your mouth. Where would they have taken her?"

All bravado had evaporated from Lauer. His face went from crimson to pasty in a matter of seconds. His jaw dropped open as he peered around Drake to Rink.

For his part, Rink made sure Lauer got a good look at the wrench in his hand.

"Taken who?" Lauer asked. His voice was just above a whisper.

Drake shrugged. "Have it your way."

He turned and nodded to Rink.

Rink stepped onto the porch in one bound. He held the wrench by his side and went straight for Lauer. "Knee or elbow?"

"Oh Jesus," Lauer said. "What are you doing? You can't do this! People will see, they'll call the police."

Rink bore down on him and drew the wrench back.

Lauer crumpled to the ground in front of them. Tears streamed down his face. "You assholes couldn't just listen to me, could you?"

Rink paused. Looked a question to Drake.

Drake gave a tiny shake of the head and stepped forward. "Listened about what?"

Lauer remained on his knees. Folded his arms in tight across his stomach. "I knew what you were talking about the second you showed up here on Sunday. Why do you think I acted that way? I was trying to protect you!"

"Protect us?" Drake asked. "By keeping us in the dark? Not telling us who the hell we were up against?"

"Because you were better off not knowing," Lauer said. "Can't you see that? I knew this would happen if you kept digging!"

Drake looked at Rink, jerked his head towards Lauer.

Rink got the message. He stepped forward and positioned the wrench just inches in front of his prey's nose.

"How? How did you know?" Drake asked. "Were you in on it?"

Lauer opened his mouth to answer, got as far as the wrench staring back at him. Choked out a couple of unintelligible words.

"How, dammit?" Drake snapped.

"No, no no no," Lauer said, shaking his head. "They came to me a long time ago. They needed a lawyer, asked if I wanted in. Said they would fabricate some pictures and show them to my wife if I didn't join them."

"So you did it?" Drake asked.

"No!" Lauer shouted. "I have kids of my own, I couldn't be part of that. The assholes still ended my marriage anyway. Stop by every now and again to make sure I haven't told anybody."

Drake leaned back. Cast a glance to Rink.

"Why do you think I took you guys to see that adoption hearing?" Lauer whispered. "They make me go. Make me watch. Remind me that my kids will be next if I ever say a word to anybody."

Drake nodded. For some reason, he believed Lauer's story. Something about the raw emotion he used when telling it.

It was too personal to be fake.

"Where?" Drake asked.

Lauer raised his eyes. He tried to look at Drake, got a good view of the wrench instead.

"Where? Drake repeated.

"I don't know," Lauer said. "I swear to God I don't know where they'd take her."

Rink drew the wrench back again. Aimed it at the man's exposed right shoulder.

Lauer cringed and rolled down onto his side. "I don't know! I swear! They have a compound down in the Bitterroot, right off the highway. That's where they take the girls. They'd kill me if they found out I even know that."

"How *do* you know that?" Drake pressed.

"Riley Bennett, the attorney from the hearing, was drunk and told me one night. I doubt that's where they'd take her, but that's all I know. I swear on my kid's lives, that's all I know!"

After the last word, his body pulled itself into the fetal position.

Drake looked again at Rink. Tossed his head towards the truck.

There was nothing more for them to get here.

Rink tapped the wrench on the ground once more for effect and watched as Lauer cringed.

Together, the two of them walked off the porch and back to the truck.

Behind them, Lauer remained curled tight into a ball on the ground, sobbing.

Chapter Forty-Nine

Variety is the spice of life.

A cliché to be sure, but for some reason it had always resonated with Notch. Something about its purist simplicity.

And the fact that it was absolutely, unquestionably, correct.

Behind him, the girl lay face up on an oversized wooden workbench. Her limbs were spread wide into an X, her wrists and ankles secured with links of baling twine.

She was sedated, but only a little. He didn't want her squirming or screaming.

Did want her cognizant of everything that was going on.

A pile of miscellaneous tools and paint cans lay off to the side. When they'd arrived an hour before, Notch had cleared the table with one swipe of his arm.

The barn was the last tangible remnant of his parents. The only thing of any value they'd left him on the small parcel of land high in the hills north of town.

The only thing after he'd burned the house to the ground the very night they died anyway.

They always did say they wanted to be cremated. Seemed foolish to pay someone else to do it.

The girl lay with her head to the side, staring right at him. Her eyes looked clear and unblinking, but he knew they were fuzzy at best.

He didn't need her to see everything that was about to happen. Just needed her to feel it.

It wasn't any fun for him unless he knew they felt it.

The girl released a string of mumbles just loud enough to draw his attention. The words were all unintelligible. A line of drool ran from her mouth.

"Slow down, baby," Notch said. He smiled for his own benefit, not hers. "We've got to make your boyfriend sweat. Drag this out until the wee hours of dawn."

The girl tried to choke out some more words. Her shoulder twitched as if she were trying to flee.

The combination of twine and drugs kept her from moving even an inch.

"Oh, alright. Have it your way," Notch said and looked down at the selection of toys he had brought, all lined up on a tarp.

The arrangement made him think of himself like a surgeon readying for a procedure.

Notch stood with his arms folded across his chest for a moment. Pondered the assortment of goodies spread out in front of him.

He needed something that would bring about excruciating pain. Would leave a mark.

More than that though, he needed something that she could survive until morning.

His eyes lingered on a blow torch on the far right side of the spread. Flicked over to a pair of pliers still bearing crusted blood from just a week before.

A smile grew on his face.

"I wonder," Notch said aloud, "how attached are you to your toenails?"

The girl's eyes grew a fraction wider. Again her shoulder shrugged against the table.

A string of garble and saliva spewed from her face.

Notch drowned it all out with the sound of lighting the blowtorch.

Chapter Fifty

Drake slid back into the passenger seat of the truck and used the tail of his shirt to wipe sweat from his forehead.

"We heading out there?" Rink asked as he folded himself behind the wheel and pulled the truck away from the curb in front of Lauer's house.

The wrench sat on the front bench seat between him and Ella. She didn't seem to notice.

"No," Drake said. "Drop me off in front of the rec center."

Rink made a face. "Say what?"

"I can't ask you to go out there," Drake said.

"You didn't," Rink said. He didn't need to add that he was volunteering, maybe even demanding, to make the trip.

"Not with her in tow," Drake said.

Rink started to reply, but stopped short. Snorted in agreement.

"Besides, we have no idea what's out there. I doubt they have her there. Might just be a group of pregnant girls sitting around watching TV."

"You really believe that?"

Drake remained silent, watched as the law school came into view. Rink maneuvered them past it and pulled to a stop in front of the rec.

"I'll call you as soon as I know anything," Drake said. He jumped from the truck and hit the ground running without waiting for a response.

He went inside just long enough to hit the locker room. He changed back into his black t-shirt and used the one he was wearing to towel off once more.

Opted to remain in the gym shorts and running shoes.

Something told him they might be more effective than flip-flops and jeans.

Five minutes after jumping from Rink's truck, he climbed into his own. He aimed it towards the south end of town and laid on the gas.

The early evening traffic was thin and allowed him to move through it with ease. Off to his right, the sun began its descent below the horizon. The temperature was starting to drop, but his entire body was bathed in sweat.

The directions Lauer gave him were simple enough to follow. There was only road that led south into the Bitterroot Valley, and it was a highway.

Shortly after leaving campus, he left the edge of Missoula behind. Just ten minutes after that, he slowed his truck and made a left turn into an unmarked driveway.

Just like Lauer said.

Drake felt his pulse quicken as he pulled the truck back the gravel lane. He wrapped around a small bend in the path and behind him the highway disappeared. Even the sound of it fell away.

A hundred thoughts raced through his head as a cluster of buildings appeared.

What was he doing here? What would he do if he found Ava? How far was he willing to go to protect her?

From the moment he'd gotten the call atop the mountain, he'd been moving with blind energy. For the first time in a couple of hours, he could actually see what he was doing playing out in front of him.

What he was doing was very stupid.

Rink and possibly Lauer were the only two people on earth that knew where he was. There could be at least one, maybe many, psychopaths waiting for him.

He couldn't call the police. They were involved.

He couldn't call his friends. He didn't want them any more involved.

Drake gripped the steering wheel tightly. Forced himself to breath. Watched as the buildings grew closer.

The lane ended in a small turnabout in front of a single level house. Off to the side was two smaller buildings connected by a breezeway.

"Main headquarters, bunk houses for the girls," Drake whispered.

Only a single car sat in the driveway. An older SUV with bumper stickers that read **Montana Tech Miners** and **Butte, America**.

Even in the waning evening light, he could tell the house was void of life.

"Cars gone, lights out," Drake mumbled. "Nobody's home."

Drake pulled the truck to a stop just past the front door, left it facing the road in case he needed to make a quick getaway.

There was no chance Ava was here. Still, he had no other options. He had to go inside and see what he could find.

Drake left the keys in the ignition and climbed out. He barely clicked the door closed and moved in long bounds across the gravel driveway onto the front sidewalk.

Paused and listened.

There was no sound.

Breathing hard, he stepped to the front door and checked the knob. Found it open and slid inside.

Just like with the truck, he left it cracked open behind him. Stood on the front foyer and listened for any sound.

To his left was an oversized living room. Standard arrangement of furniture and television.

In front of him extended a hallway. He could see a large kitchen at the end of it. Pots and pans hung from hooks along the ceiling. A small lamp was on above the oven, but there was no movement of any kind.

Off to the right was a room bathed in eerie grey light. Drake stepped towards it and found a bank of television monitors displaying various views of the grounds.

His heart began to pound even harder.

Lauer was right to use the word compound. Every square inch of the place was being monitored.

Beneath the screens was a wide desk and two computer CPU's to record the footage. A black leather desk chair set empty in front of everything.

Drake rose onto the balls of his feet and shuffled into the room. He rifled through the drawers in the desk and checked each of the shelves on a small wall unit in the back.

There was no paper of any kind in the room. Not just anything that would give him a clue where Ava might be.

Nothing, period.

Whoever these people were, they were efficient. And paranoid as hell.

Frustrated, Drake gave up on the room and turned his attention to the monitors. Maybe there was somebody on the grounds that could help him.

The top row consisted of views within the house. The kitchen. The living room. A pair of bedrooms. Even the room he now stood in.

The rest of the house looked normal. If there was nothing of value in this room, there was nothing anywhere inside.

The second row displayed the rear of the grounds. A deck with split log furniture. A fire pit. A boat landing for fishing the river.

The third row showed the other buildings he'd seen when driving up. The first two screens showed a room of empty beds. Assorted clothes and gear were strewn about.

The place was in use, but vacant for the time being.

The last two screens showed an exact replica of the first bunkhouse. Two even rows of beds with clothing and such thrown about.

The only difference was the half dozen girls interspersed among them.

Drake felt his breath catch in his throat. "They'll know where he has her," he whispered aloud.

He didn't bother to check the last two rows of camera feeds. He turned on his heel and headed for the front door. Eased out and closed it behind him.

The sound of a man clearing his throat stopped him where he stood.

Slowly, Drake turned to face the driveway.

Six men, all weighing at least forty more pounds than he did, stared back at him.

"Oh shit."

Chapter Fifty-One

The girl was easier to break than Notch anticipated.

He'd started on her left foot. Removed her big toe nail first and watched her body feeble attempts to thrash about.

Seared the gaping hole closed with the blow torch and watched her squirm some more.

Saliva poured from her mouth. Tears streamed from her eyes.

By the second toenail, she was unconscious.

Notch considered finishing the foot while she was out, but decided against it. He hated leaving anything undone. At the same time, he hated his victims not experiencing every excruciating second of his work.

A master likes to be appreciated.

Years of practice had taught him it was better to wait an hour or so before reviving a victim. Any sooner, and the pain is too raw. They'll just go right back under.

Instead, he put his tools back into place on the tarp. Settled into a fold-out chair and waited.

It was a short wait.

Ten minutes after he was done with the girl's second toe, the sound of tires on gravel caught his attention. He left everything in the room as it was and picked up a machete from the spread of implements on the floor.

Within seconds, he'd melted into the shadows of the room.

The sound of footsteps filtered in. A moment later, the barn door swung open.

Yelena emerged, followed by Mayor Sloan.

Both made faces as they did so. Raised forearms to their noses and looked like they may vomit at any moment.

"Notch?" Yelena called.

Notch paused to make sure they were alone before stepping out from the corner of the room. He tapped the machete against the front of his jeans as he went.

A little reminder that he'd heard them coming. Could have done anything he wanted the moment they walked in.

"What *the hell* is that smell?" Mayor Sloan asked.

Notch jerked his head towards the table. "Let's just say our friend won't be dancing any time soon."

Yelena made another face and looked past Notch to the table. "You're a sick man, you know that?"

The same sadistic smile met the comment. "Isn't that why you hired me?"

As best Notch could tell, it *was* the reason they'd hired him.

How they got his name was still a mystery to him. Something inside told him he should care a little more, but he just couldn't bring himself to do it.

It was no secret that he'd had a reputation since he was a kid. Started when he used to torture neighborhood pets.

When word got out, his parents moved him to the country away from town. It didn't help. Instead of hunting cats with a slingshot, he started walking the woods at night, hunting bears with a gun on either hip.

By the time he was an adult, the stories around town had taken on a life of their own. People began to speak of him in hushed whispers, started referring to him as Notch.

The part he always found amusing was that despite the whispers, the people couldn't begin to fathom all the things he'd done. If they could, they'd have come up with something a lot worse to call him.

"Why are you here?" Notch said. "Come to make sure I didn't kill her?"

Yelena's face remained twisted, as if trying to block the smell of charred flesh. "The plot has thickened."

"What the hell's that supposed to mean?"

Mayor Sloan held up a cell-phone and wagged it from side to side. "We were at a campaign dinner. Got a message that the house has been breached."

"How do you know?"

"The front door is always unlocked," Yelena said, "but the silent alarm is on whenever we're not there. It sends a message right to our phones."

"Maybe one of your breeders did it."

"The girls know better," Mayor Sloan said.

"Maybe one your new goons did it," Notch said, contempt plain in his voice.

He could tell by their reactions they were surprised he knew about the hired hands.

"They...they were also told to stay out," Yelena managed.

Notch snorted. Walked over, dropped the machete back into place and straightened it with the toe of his boot.

"So have them handle it," Notch said.

"They will," Mayor Sloan said, "that's not the point."

"Then what is?" Notch asked. "If you haven't noticed, I'm a little tied up at the moment. Well, *she's* tied up, but you get the idea."

"The point is, if this kid can find us, anybody can," Yelena said.

"And what? Call the Sheriff?"

Yelena and Mayor Sloan exchanged a glance. Both pushed out long, slow breaths.

Outside, the sound of another car approaching could be heard.

Notch eyes narrowed. "Who else did you call?"

"Everybody," Yelena said. "We have a leak somewhere. It needs to be plugged."

For the first time, the intent of their visit dawned on Notch. Suddenly, he found himself rife with anticipation.

"And I get to plug it?" he asked.

Mayor Sloan cast a disgusted look to the girl lying unconscious on the table. "If it comes to that."

Chapter Fifty-Two

"Oh shit is right," one of the guys said. He stood left center of the group, took a half step forward.

Asserted himself as the leader.

Even across the open expanse of gravel between them, Drake could see the guy was maybe an inch taller than him, about fifty pounds heavier.

He shifted his eyes around the group.

Heights ranging from five-ten to six-three. Weights going from two-forty to three bills or more.

He caught the sight of his truck in his peripheral vision. Considered it for a moment. He had no doubt he could get there before they could.

Considerable doubt that he could get it started and out the drive before they caught up.

Adrenaline surged through his body. His pulse and breathing both quickened.

He'd been in a fight before. More than one.

Just never six on one. Never outweighed probably eight to one.

Drake considered throwing out one of the canned lines that people in movies use in these situations.

You don't have to do this.

We can talk this out.

Nobody has to know.

It was evident though that these guys weren't here to talk. Some of them looked like they might not even be able to talk.

Drake made a decision. There was no doubt he was about to catch a beating. If he was lucky, he'd might be able to walk away from it.

If he wasn't, he would damned sure go down swinging.

"You think you brought enough guys?" Drake asked. He rocked up onto the balls of his feet, prepared himself to spring forward.

The lead man smiled and extended his arms to either side. "I never go anywhere without my crew."

Behind him, the sky lightened. A persistent orb of light that seemed to grow with each passing second.

It was close enough to make Drake pause. There was no way this was good. Best case, somebody would call off the dogs. Worst case, they would have something worse in store for him.

The light grew larger fast. Pulled up in front of the bunkhouse and slid to a stop, throwing gravel everywhere.

The lights remained on as a trio of shadows emerged before them.

Ajax. Kade. Rink.

The lead guy turned and squinted into the headlights. "Who the hell are you?"

"They're *my* crew," Drake said as he launched himself at the guy. He buried his shoulder into soft stomach and pulled the legs beneath it in tight. Lifted and drove him into the ground.

Perfect form tackle.

Air rushed out from the man as Drake popped to knee and snapped two straight rights into his nose.

Around him, he could hear grunts, yells. A cacophony of pain from the goon squad. Of angry muttering and yelling from the Crew.

Drake pulled back for a third punch and felt two strong hands grab hold and jerk him backwards.

Out of pure reflex he forced his elbow back as hard as he could and felt the wind rush out of his attacker. Spun around and buried his knee into the guy's doubled-over face.

Stepped forward and swung a kick across the leader's jaw.

With crazed intensity, he tossed his gaze around the lot in search of his next target.

There was none.

Opposite him, Kade and Ajax both stood over inert bodies.

Rink was crouched over another. He threw a wicked right-left-right into the guy's face, stood and wiped the blood from his target's nose on to his jeans.

For a moment all four stood in silence. Stared down at the group of six lying sprawled out in the gravel.

Not one of them so much as moved.

Drake was the first to break the silence. No canned lines. Nothing scripted.

Just, simply, "Thanks."

Chapter Fifty-Three

The entire group filed in together.

From the opposite side, it may have looked like some sort of contrived attempt at a show of force.

To them, it was merely a strength-in-numbers kind of thing. They all knew Notch was a loose cannon. Figured, hoped, he might be less apt to try anything on them as a group.

Individually, there was no chance any of them could match him. Maybe, standing there five across, they could at least dissuade him from even trying.

In truth, they had no idea why they'd been summoned to a barn in the middle of the night. Based on what happened the previous Sunday and what was going on around them, they knew it couldn't be good.

Odds were, someone was about to be killed. They all just hoped it was somebody outside their group without actually saying as much.

Sheriff Spore went first. His hand wasn't on his weapon as he entered, but the snap on his holster was undone. It could be drawn at a moment's notice.

Dr. Schievers went next, followed by Harken in the middle. Judge Tanner and Bennett made up the rear. They filed in as a tight bunch and stood along the back wall.

All tried to keep from vomiting at the stench in the room.

Off to the side was Yelena and Mayor Sloan. Both looked just as repulsed and held their arms folded tight over their stomachs.

Across from everyone stood Notch. A canvas tarp was spread out on the ground beside him, various implements laid out in even rows atop it.

Behind him, a young woman was tied to a wooden table. She appeared to be unconscious, the source of the foul odor in the air.

None of them noticed her though. What they noticed was what Notch was holding.

A ball pein hammer in one hand. A machete in the other.

Between the tension and the stench, it was difficult for anyone to breath.

"What's this all about?" Sheriff Spore asked, cast his gaze between the ladies and Notch.

Silence met his question for several long seconds.

"I think you know," Notch replied. Smiled.

All five people fidgeted. None had any idea what he was referring to.

Yelena let them squirm for almost a full minute as she tried to determine if anyone seemed extra nervous.

Nobody stood out any more than the others.

"We've had a breach," Mayor Sloan said.

"What kind of breach?" Dr. Schievers asked.

"Someone showed up at the compound tonight," Yelena said. "Very much uninvited."

"Shouldn't have even known where it was, let alone had the gall to show up," Mayor Sloan added.

"Who?" Bennett asked. "What were they looking for?"

Yelena started to respond. Notch beat her to it.

"You tell us." He said it in a graveled voice just above a whisper. Everybody heard it anyway.

Five jaws dropped open at once.

"Is that why we're here?" Judge Tanner asked. "You think one of us tipped them off? And this is some sort of shakedown?"

Notch twisted his head to the side. Tapped the flat blade of the machete against his thigh.

Judge Tanner turned away from Notch, focused on Yelena and Mayor Sloan.

"You have got to be kidding me. Like I said on Sunday, we're all in. You've got your hooks into us."

"And do you really think if any one of us had sent someone out to the compound, we'd be standing here right now?" Dr. Schievers added and held his arms out to his side. "Look around, we're all here. Walked in under our own volition."

Yelena and Mayor Sloan exchanged a glance.

"Only one way to be sure," Notch said. He continued to dangle the weapons from either hand.

All five remained motionless. Held their breath and waited.

In one fluid motion, Notch pivoted on the ball of his foot, raised the hammer into the air and smashed it down into the lower half of the girl's left leg.

The impact made a sickening crack that filled the room. The girl's body jerked against its bindings, fell back against the table.

Yelena and Mayor Sloan both turned away.

Harken yelped.

The others all winced.

"Now," Notch said, "is there anything else you all would like to tell us? Because that was a warning shot. If I have to come after one of you, that will look like a love tap."

Yelena and Mayor Sloan both turned back to face him. Their faces were pale.

Yelena opened her mouth to speak.

Notch cut her off again. Extended the hammer in her direction. "You shut the hell up. You brought this on yourself, bringing in extra help. Didn't think I was up to the task anymore?

"I'll show you how damn up to it I am."

He took half a step towards the sisters, his weapons readied by his side.

"You brought in help?" Bennett asked from across the room.

Notch stopped and turned to face the others. All five of them were staring at Yelena and Mayor Sloan.

"Who are they? Why weren't we consulted?" Bennett pressed.

"Just some extra muscle, nobody important," Mayor Sloan snapped.

"And we don't have to *consult* you on a damn thing," Yelena added. "You work for us."

Bennett fell silent.

Beside him, Judge Tanner said, "So then they should have taken care of the intruders, right?"

Notch snorted.

Yelena and Mayor Sloan looked at each other. Said nothing.

"So then there isn't a problem?" Judge Tanner asked.

"The problem," Yelena said, "isn't if our guys took care of things. I'm sure they did. The problem is that there was anything to take care of."

"Nobody outside this room is supposed to know about the house," Mayor Sloan.

"We've shuffled a dozen girls or more through there," Sheriff Spore said. "It could have been anybody."

"Hell, I assume that's why she's laying over there?" Bennett added. "Or what about, I don't know, the pregnant one you guys seem to have lost?"

Again silence fell.

"There's no way any of them would talk," Yelena seethed. "They know better. They know we'd kill them and everyone they know."

“Besides, none of them are within a thousand miles of this place,” Mayor Sloan added.

"I thought right now we can't even find the missing girl?" Dr. Schievers asked. No condemnation at all in his voice. Very much a flat question. "She could be anywhere. They have to be connected, right?"

More silence.

Yelena and Mayor Sloan exchanged another glance, a mixture of uncertainty and disgust.

"Of course they are," Notch said. "That's why I have this girl here now. She knows, and she *will* talk."

Bennett turned his gaze to the young girl lying on the table, to her left leg distended at a grotesque angle from the rest of her body.

"How the hell is she going to do that now?"

Notch stared long and hard at the entire row for several moments. He walked back to the tarp and dropped the machete onto it.

He slid a pink cell-phone from his pocket and held it up for all to see.

"She doesn't have to."

Chapter Fifty-Four

Adrenaline.

The common street name for epinephrine. A hormone and neurotransmitter critical to regulating the body's nervous system.

Most notable, taking the normal docile self and elevating it into a fight-or-flight response.

In this instance, it had lifted Drake and the Crew into fighting.

"How'd you know?" Drake asked as he released his fists. His head continued moving, checking to make sure each of their opponents remained immobile.

"Because you didn't have a choice but to come here," Rink said.

He was right. Drake didn't have a choice. Under normal circumstances, he would never go on a fool's errand like running blind into a compound.

All things considered, these were far from normal circumstances.

Drake turned his eyes to Kade. "When'd you get back?"

"Sage called on her way to work. Said some shit was going down, I needed to be here."

"Beth?"

"She's safe," Kade said, nodded his head for emphasis.

That was good enough for Drake. He didn't need to press any further.

"Again, thanks," Drake repeated.

"Did you find her?" Rink asked.

"No."

"Then don't thank us yet."

Drake nodded. Again, he was right.

"What's next?" Ajax asked.

Drake swallowed in a deep gulp of air and felt the adrenaline ebb from his system. For the first time he noticed the cool evening breath blowing across his body.

"There are some girls in the bunkhouse over there," Drake said. "I was on my way to go ask them where they'd take her when these guys showed up."

"So go ask them," Kade said. "We'll clean this up."

Drake nodded. Resisted the urge to thank them again for fear at this point it might only offend them.

"Ajax, there's a room off to the right inside the house. Full of surveillance equipment, some other computers and stuff. Didn't seem like anything to me. Maybe you can get something from it?"

"I'll take a look," Ajax said. He walked past Drake and on into the house.

Drake took off in the opposite direction across the open gravel, walking fast. Behind him he could hear Kade and Rink start lugging the bodies around, grunting and cursing.

He approached the door to the bunkhouse and considered for just a moment how to proceed. The monitors had showed him at least a handful of girls were inside. He would like to believe they were like Beth and see him as a friend, but what if they didn't?

What if he was walking into a Stockholm Syndrome fueled hornet's nest?

He paused outside the door and drew in another breath.

There was no time for uncertainty. Somewhere, Ava was in trouble.

Drake knocked twice with the back of his hand. There was no knob on the door, so he pushed inside and was bathed in bright light.

An empty room stared back at him.

He did a quick scan of the place. Nothing unusual. No imminent danger apparent.

"I'm not going to hurt you," he said aloud. He took a few steps into the room and raised his hands by his side. "I am in no way affiliated with whoever's been keeping you here."

Again, more silence.

"I'm a friend of Beth's."

Those seemed to be the magic words. At once, six faces appeared from around the room. They peeked from beneath beds, emerging from a chest, even a closet.

Of the six, there was an even split of blonde and brunette. All looked to be younger than he was, ranging from maybe twenty to twenty-four.

None wore makeup. All had simple ponytails.

All between four and eight months pregnant.

"So she's okay?" a blonde closest to him asked.

"She's safe," Drake replied.

A few of the girls sighed. The others remained passive, stared at him.

"I need your help," Drake said.

The blonde turned to the others. Looked back at him. "Who are you?"

"My name is Drake. I was a friend of Beth's in college, I'm now a lawyer." A small lie. He didn't feel the need to correct it. "She asked me to help her, to help all of you."

"You can't help us," a brunette in the back said.

"I can," Drake assured her. "But right now I need you to help me. Please."

"What do you need?" the blonde asked.

"They have my friend Ava. They're holding her until they get Beth back. Doing God knows what to her."

Three pairs of eyes slid shut. A tear slid down the brunette's cheek.

The girls had witnessed firsthand what they could do.

"That's awful," a brunette to his left whispered. "You don't want to know what they're capable of."

A shudder passed over Drake. "You're right. I don't. I'm trying to stop anything at all from happening to her. I just need to know where she is."

The blonde took back over. "We want to help, but we can't. If she's not here, we have no idea."

"There's no place else? No place you've heard them talk about? Seen them," he hated to even say the word, "torture in the past?"

The brunette to the left replied, "That was only once. They blindfolded us and drove us out there."

Drake cursed under his breath. He stood with his hands on his hips thinking for another second.

"Alright, grab whatever you can carry. We're getting out of here."

"Where are we going?" the blonde asked.

"Someplace safe," Drake said. Made a twirling motion with his hand. "Come on. Outside, two minutes."

He left the girls to gather their things. He stepped out of the room to find Kade and Rink had piled the thugs into a loose circle and tied them up using rappelling line from Rink's truck.

"Anything?" Rink said.

Drake shook his head. "No. Six girls, but they keep them in the dark."

Ajax stepped out from the front door and walked across the gravel to join them. "Nothing on the computer either, it was just a database for the cameras. Pulled some interesting head shots from them though."

He held up his cell-phone and extended it for the group to see.

"Is that who I think it is...?" Drake asked, letting his voice trail off.

"The one and only Mayor Maria Sloan," Kade said. "And to think I voted for her ass."

"Voted? Hell, I donated to her campaign," Ajax said.

Drake passed a hand over his face. "No wonder Beth said no police. The whole damn town's in on it."

Behind them, the girls streamed out from the bunkhouse, all still dressed in pajamas and athletic shoes. Most clutched book bags or purses against their chests.

"What are we going to do with them?" Rink asked.

Drake gave a twist of his head. "We've still got the room at the Hawthorne, right?"

The group mulled the suggestion for a moment in silence.

Ajax nodded his approval. "I wouldn't keep them there long-term or nothing, but it could work for the night."

Drake glanced to Rink. "Half in your truck, half in mine?"

Rink nodded. The group turned as one and started to direct the girls where to go.

They were interrupted halfway through by a call to Drake's phone.

Ava.

Chapter Fifty-Five

Drake went rigid.

Everybody, the Crew and the girls, noticed. All of them fell silent. They stood as one and waited for a sign, any sign, from him.

His heart pounded in his chest. By now whoever was on the line had to know he was there. They might even be watching.

"Hello?"

"I take it the new *added muscle* was no trouble for you?"

Same cold, graveled voice. A tone that insinuated the message wasn't just aimed at him.

Drake thought for a moment and decided not to let Notch dictate the direction of the conversation. Opted for the offensive approach.

"Where's Ava?"

"She's here," Notch said. "Trust me. She's not going anywhere."

Drake balled his off hand into a fist. Squeezed until he could feel his fingernails digging into the palm.

Still, he pushed aside the urge to walk into the trap and fire some stupid threat, something hollow about the man not hurting her.

It was clear he had already hurt her. Whatever Drake did now might determine how much worse it got.

"What do you want?"

Notch laughed. "You're a fast learner. Already you're doing better than the last time we talked."

"What do you want?"

The laughter died away. The same hard edge appeared in Notch's voice. "What do you think I want? I want the damn girl and I want you to disappear."

"And in return?"

"In return, I might not kill you all."

The words dripped with malevolence. Drake could tell Notch believed every last one of them, would go to the ends of the earth to make them a reality.

Deep breath.

With eyes closed, Drake offered a prayer that what he was about to say might not get Ava killed.

"You're going to have to do better than that."

Another harsh crack of laughter bit back into his ear. "I have your girlfriend tied to a table right now. You think you're in any position to negotiate?"

"I have your about-to-burst surrogate stashed nearby," Drake replied. "I'd say that makes for an even trade."

Notch snorted. "I'm about to take back my earlier comment. You got balls kid, but you ain't got a lick of brains."

"Maybe not," Drake said. "Do we have a deal?"

Notch paused and drew in a long breath. "Alright. Yeah, we've got a deal. You load that pregnant cow up and bring her over here. We'll trade."

"And where is here?"

"Shelbourne Road, north of town. You know the place?"

"I've got GPS."

"Alright then, you and your GPS get your ass up here. There's a barn off a dirt lane at the very end. Bring the bitch. Nobody else. You have an hour."

Drake didn't like the idea of a ticking clock over his head. Wanted at least a couple hours so he could devise a plan. Maybe scout the situation a little.

"I don't think I can make it there in an hour," Drake said.

"Then you better drive fast," Notch said. "Otherwise I'll make sure nobody ever sees your girlfriend again."

The line went dead.

Drake kept it pressed to his face for several more seconds before lowering it. He didn't even realize he'd been staring at the group the entire time.

"What's up?" Kade asked and took a slow step forward. Beside him, Ajax did the same.

Drake swallowed hard. Blinked himself out of the phone call. "He gave me an address where they're keeping Ava. Shelbourne Road, in an old barn."

"I know that road," Kade said. "I've hunted up there. I can drive."

Drake shook his head. "He said to load Beth up and come alone."

"There's no way in hell you're going there alone," Ajax said. "It's a trap."

"I know," Drake said.

"And besides, there's no chance at getting Beth there in an hour," Kade said.

Drake turned his head to face him. "How far away is she?"

He didn't ask where. If he needed to know, Kade would have told him already.

Kade twisted his face for a moment. Considered the question. Shook his head from side to side.

There was no way he could have Beth there in time.

"Shit," Drake mumbled and looked around the group once more.

On one side stood the Crew. All three amped up, ready to fight. All ready to do anything he asked of them.

On the other side stood six girls. All but the blonde and the second brunette looked at the ground. Hugged their packs. Avoided eye contact.

Drake pushed out a heavy breath. "Let's start by getting these girls out of here." He looked at the blonde. "Can you drive?"

She didn't answer the question.

What she did say was even more profound.

"I can be Beth."

Chapter Fifty-Six

Her name was Angie.

The brunette, that is.

Drake gave her the keys to his truck and sent her and the other four girls to The Hawthorne. Told them to draw the curtains, lock the doors.

Do not open for anyone until they heard his voice.

The girls resembled a flock of frightened geese as they shuffled into his truck. All remained pressed tight together and continued to avoid eye contact.

The sound of the truck starting and the lights turning on stirred some of the guys tied up on the ground.

At first there was nothing but muffled moans. A few attempts to move. After a minute or two, they began asking to be untied, tossing out excuses about how they'd just been hired that morning and had no idea what was really going on.

The Crew ignored them.

The blonde tried to give them her name too. Drake waved her off. "For the next couple of hours, it's Beth. Better that we only know that and don't mess it up."

"So we're going too?" Ajax asked.

"You don't think for a second he's going alone do you?" Kade countered.

"Not a chance," Rink agreed.

Together all five piled into the truck. Rink, the new Beth, Drake in the front. Ajax and Kade in the bed.

A cold ride for sure, but still better than the five of them squeezed into the cab.

Rink sat behind the wheel and angled them in the direction Kade pointed out before departing. For several long minutes, the cab was silent.

Drake thinking hard. Rink gripping the steering wheel. 'Beth' taking in measured breaths.

"How far along are you?" Drake asked. He kept his eyes on the windshield in front of him, watched as they wheeled through town and headed back out into the country.

"Thirty weeks."

"Will they notice?" Drake asked.

"If they looked maybe," the girl whispered. "Beth is due any day now. She's bigger than all of us."

"Do you have a blanket or anything in here?" Drake asked.

"Got some old drop cloths in the back," Rink said. "How you looking to handle this?"

"I'm thinking we'll stop just before we get there. Wrap her up in one. Let some of her blonde hair hang out. Make it big and baggy on her."

"So they can't see her face or the size of her stomach," Rink said.

Drake continued without acknowledging. "She and I will go in on foot. You guys hang back a few minutes. Make sure nobody's outside. I'll give you the whistle when it's time to enter."

He didn't need to elaborate on the whistle. Everybody that knew him knew it, as did everybody that lived within a two block radius of him.

The plan was thin. At best. They all knew it.

Nobody commented on it.

Drake would have welcomed any feedback they had. He just figured, like him, they knew they were in trouble.

They had a very small window between bringing in the girl and the other side realizing she was a fake Beth. Drake somehow had to get inside, grab Ava, hope that he and The Crew could get everyone out.

It was a pure suicide mission.

Rink nodded behind the wheel and lowered his voice. "You know, I don't have but one gun in here. And it's a .9mm. It was the only thing I could get over the border when I came down from Canada."

He added the last line almost as if an apology.

"If we walk into a shooting gallery..."

"I know," Drake whispered. "I don't expect anybody to get shot over this. You hear any gunfire, get the guys, get Beth, get the hell out of there."

"We won't leave you."

Drake knew they wouldn't. Knew no amount of arguing with them would change it.

"Still, if things go bad, don't be afraid to cut bait and go."

Rink said nothing.

Outside, the city lights receded behind them. Heavy darkness settled in.

Rink pushed the truck up over seventy miles an hour and followed the directions Kade gave them to the letter.

Forty minutes after leaving the compound, they found Shelbourne Road.

Five minutes after that, they found the dirt lane.

Ahead in the distance, they could see a single light through the woods.

The three of them piled out of the truck cab. Rink grabbed a drop cloth and handed it over to Drake.

Ajax and Kade both stood shivering in the bed of the truck, but said nothing.

Drake wrapped the heavy cloth around the girl. He adjusted it so her face was hidden within the deep folds of the makeshift cloak, just a few strands of blonde hair hanging down.

He gave a single nod to the Crew and hooked an arm around her. Together, they took off walking towards the single light ahead through the woods.

Chapter Fifty-Seven

Notch considered untying the girl.

Decided against it.

Thought about covering her from the waist down.

Decided against that too.

He had broken her leg to teach a lesson to the others in their organization. Nothing wrong with letting this little piss ant get that message too.

Besides, it wasn't like the kid was going to be alive long after he saw her. It didn't matter what he thought of her mangled leg.

Notch did choose to put away his tools though. He loaded them all back into his truck and wrapped the canvas over them.

Kept out an extendable night stick and a meat tenderizer. Slid a flap jack into the butt pocket of his jeans.

He stowed everything else away and pulled the truck to the rear of the barn.

While he worked, the others milled together near the front door. Many whispered amongst themselves. They all avoided eye contact.

Years of practice had taught him the best way to maintain their fear was to act like they weren't even there. Go about his business and let them know their presence was of no consequence to him.

Even without looking, he could tell it was working.

Once he was done, he checked the girl's cell-phone and walked back into the middle of the room. He didn't bother to motion to the others, just launched into talking without warning.

"Here's how it's going to go. I told him to come alone. He knows it's a trap, but he also knows I'll kill the girl unless he does what I say. He'll come alone.

"You four," he motioned to the four men in the room, "I want split on either side of the door. When he walks in, block his exit."

Notch turned away from the group and walked back to the table still positioned in the middle of the room.

"Then what happens?" Bennett asked.

Notch stopped walking, turned, gave a look that was pure venom. "Then one of you grabs the girl and I go to work on him.

When it's all over, we take some pictures of him," he motioned to the girl on the table, "and her. Make sure this kind of thing never happens again."

Every one of the men looked like they may vomit. None of them voiced objection.

It was a shame too. Notch was kind of hoping one of them would be dumb enough to.

"What about us?" Yelena asked, motioning to herself, her sister, Harken.

Notch smirked and pointed to the far wall.

"You three just stand over there. Stay out of the way. Try not to do anything stupid."

Harken wilted. Mayor Sloan's jaw dropped open. Yelena's face grew red. She raised a finger to fire back at him.

Notch cut her off before she had a chance to speak. "Shh."

He cocked an ear towards the front door.

"They're coming."

Chapter Fifty-Eight

"You don't have to do this," Drake whispered.

The barn loomed just a few yards away. The closer they got, the more apprehension welled within him. Not for his own well-being, but for the girl beside him.

He couldn't shake the feeling that he wasn't walking out of there alive. He'd been foolish to think anything different.

Flat stupid to lead someone else right into it with him.

"I have to go in," Drake continued. "They have my friend. It's my fault she's involved at all. You they don't know. You can still walk away."

"I volunteered for this, remember?" the girl replied, a surprising amount of conviction in her voice.

"Why?" Drake said. "Were you friends with Beth?"

"You didn't see what they did to that girl last weekend," she said simply.

Drake nodded. Point taken.

A single bare light bulb hung down from the side of the barn and threw pale yellow light over the entrance. They were just ten yards away and closing.

"Alright, you heard the plan back there," Drake said. "It's weak, we all know it. I can tell you though I will *not* leave you behind. Neither will any of the others."

"I know," the girl whispered.

Drake's running shoes padded over the dirt driveway. His periphery picked up no less than five cars parked off to the side in the darkness.

There were a lot more people waiting for him inside than anticipated. More adrenaline and apprehension surged through him.

This could get ugly fast.

Their pace picked up as they closed the last few yards to the door and pushed their way inside without pause. They walked several feet out into the middle of the room and stopped.

Drake swung his head from side to side. The fake Beth remained with her head aimed towards the floor, drop cloth draped around her like a Druid's cloak.

If the entrance surprised anyone, they didn't show it.

The putrid smell of something burning hung in the air. It filled Drake's nostrils and tinged his eyes with moisture.

The source of it lay face up on a table in the center of the room.

A cold, searing flame sprang up behind Drake's eyes as he stared at Ava. The mutilation on her foot. Her grotesquely twisted left leg. The bindings that held her unconscious body in place.

A shiny silver mallet with a textured head lay beside her.

His fists balled so tight, the girl let out a whimper beside him. He loosened his grip, stared as a man sauntered into the room and stood beside Ava.

"It's about time we meet, wouldn't you say Mr. Bell?"

The man was just as the real Beth had described him. Dressed like a local. Someone that knew his way around the mountains, knives, guns. Long ponytail. Bad teeth, hollow eyes.

Basically, he looked like a meth addict. Only his drug was inflicting evil, not ingesting powder.

"What did you do to her?" Drake asked. Nodded his head towards Ava.

Behind him, he heard the shuffling of shoes and turned to see four men slide into place between them and the door.

He recognized three of them. The sheriff. The judge. The attorney.

This was a lot bigger than he realized. Maybe Lauer was right trying to keep them far away from it.

Still, Drake couldn't help but smirk. Despite their numbers, not one of them looked like they could hold their own in a scrap.

The Crew would blow through them in no time flat.

"We just had a little fun," Notch said. "Gave her a couple of reminders what happens when you stick your nose in our business."

"And human trafficking is your business huh?"

Notch just smiled. "Their business is making money. Mine is hurting people that interfere with that."

As Notch spoke, he motioned his head to his left.

Drake glanced over to see three women standing in a cluster. One he recognized as the child services woman from the hearing. Both of the other two looked like the mayor.

He pushed his gaze back forward. Said nothing.

Notch flicked his wrist to the side. The night stick extended from the palm of his hand to over two feet in length.

"Your girlfriend interfered. She got hurt. You and that little bitch there interfered. Now you get hurt."

Adrenaline pumped back into Drake's body. He wished he was carrying some form of weapon. Gym shorts and a t-shirt just didn't offer much opportunity to conceal anything.

He rocked up onto the balls of his feet. There was no real interest in a swap of any kind. The only thing bringing the girl along had accomplished was buying him a few minutes.

He just hoped they were enough for his friends to arrive.

Notch smiled at him. Rolled his neck back. Peered at Drake in a way that displayed how much he relished the moment.

Drake lowered his chin to his right shoulder. "When you hear me whistle, I want you to run to the left as fast as you can. Get against the wall and stay there."

The girl squeezed his hand in understanding.

Drake drew in a deep breath. He could feel apprehension rolling off of everyone in the room.

He gave the girl's hand a quick squeeze and pushed his front teeth against his bottom lip.

Forced out an ear splitting whistle that could be heard for a mile in every direction.

Chapter Fifty-Nine

Three things happened at once.

The door to the barn burst off its hinges.

It didn't just open. It didn't swing out fast into the room. It literally exploded into a blur of wood chips.

Most of them hadn't even settled as Rink came through. Kade and Ajax were both less than a foot behind him.

Drake used his hold on the fake Beth's hold to jumpstart her run for the corner. Jerked her so fast the cloak flew back off her head.

Third, Drake launched his own body forward at Notch, who stood with a look that conveyed two things at once.

The girl was not Beth, and he was going to enjoy killing Drake.

Tunnel vision set in as Drake ran straight at Notch. He didn't notice the grunts and sounds of a struggle behind him. Didn't hear fake Beth crying against the wall. Never once registered the cluster of women yelling in shrill voices across the barn.

All he saw was Notch. A sadistic son of a bitch that had hurt his friends, was intent on hurting him.

Drake ran straight ahead. He gritted his teeth and pushed a carnal groan out through them.

His eyes focused in as Notch stepped to the side and held the night stick at the ready, sized him up like a slugger waiting for a fastball.

Drake maintained his path. He waited until he was just beyond the reach of Notch, dropped to his knees and slid across the smooth concrete.

A rush of wind blew across him as Notch's swing passed just above his head.

Using the momentum, Drake lifted himself back onto his feet and stopped beside the edge of the table Ava lay on. He grabbed up the meat tenderizer and turned to face Notch.

Now he was armed, albeit with little more than a hammer. It was at least a foot shorter than what Notch was working with.

Still, it was something. A renewed surge of confidence, of burning hatred, surged through him.

Notch moved first. Using the night stick as a poker, he got Drake to shift to the side and brought in a sweeping left hook.

Drake dropped beneath the hook and swung the mallet hard at Notch's mid-section. Drew nothing but air.

He used his momentum to turn a tight circle and swung a vicious chop out across Notch's knee that connected. Heard a pained grunt as the night stick smashed into the concrete just inches from him.

Drake rose to full height and threw a left cross, followed with a jab using the head of the tenderizer.

Even moving a little stiff, Notch ducked them both and poked Drake in the ribs with the night stick.

The blow doubled him over at the waist and pushed the air from his lungs.

In a practiced move, Notch slid the flap jack from his rear pocket and swung it hard down at the exposed back of Drake's skull. A second before it connected, Drake managed to get his left hand up to block.

Took the full brunt of the blow across his balled up fist.

Spectacular pain burst through his body as the bones in his hand shattered on impact.

Drake wheezed in a deep breath and drew the hand against his chest. Retreated a few steps. Kept the mallet extended in his right hand.

Notch laughed and returned to his saunter. He was still limping slightly from the knee shot, but kept moving forward.

Flap jack in one hand, night stick in the other.

"I should be pissed about you bringing your boys, but I'm kind of glad you did. Gives me more to kill once I'm done with you."

Drake had no desire to listen to the man's mouth. To sit like wounded prey while his hunter leered over him.

He pushed himself forward and buried his shoulder into Notch's ribs. Punched at his kidneys with the head of the mallet.

Drake drove Notch halfway across the room before they landed in a heap. They rolled twice, each one fighting for dominance.

Even with one hand, Drake came out on top.

Until the flap jack found his jaw.

It wasn't a direct shot, but a glancing blow, just enough to daze him. It allowed Notch to roll him over and pin him to the ground, use the night stick to pry the meat tenderizer away.

Pinned, dazed, unable to use his left hand, Drake looked up at Notch. Did the only thing he had left at his disposal.

Spit into the man's face.

The haughty sneer from a moment before evaporated from Notch's face. Incredulity replaced it.

Without saying a word, he lifted the tenderizer high above his head. Brought it down like a lumberjack swinging an ax.

Three gunshots stopped him mid-swing.

Drake flinched at the sound of each one.

Again at the fresh blood that leaked down onto his face.

The meat tenderizer slid from Notch's hand and fell to the ground with a clang. Three blossoms of blood spread across his chest.

Bloody bubbles formed around his lips.

His hollow, icy blue eyes rolled up into his head. He slouched to the side without a sound.

Using his hips, Drake pushed his attacker off and sat up expecting to find Rink standing over him with his .9mm.

Instead he found someone else lying on the floor, blood pouring from his nose, smoking gun extended at arm's length.

Sheriff Spore.

Chapter Sixty

The entire room froze in place.

In the wake of the gunshots, silence seemed to envelope everything.

Drake remained seated on the concrete floor. For the first time since whistling, he stopped to look around.

Across the room, only the lady from child services remained against the wall. She was cowered down into a squatting position with her hands pressed tight over her ears, eyes jammed shut.

To the right was carnage.

Sheriff Spore was laid out flat on the ground. His upper body was propped up an elbow. Blood stained the front of his torn Sheriff's uniform.

Extended out from him, Ajax, Kade, and Rink were bent at the waist.

Ajax was hunched over the only one of the bunch Drake didn't recognize. From the looks of things, nobody else would either for a while.

Beside him was Kade. His long hair was disheveled and his shirt was rumpled. No visible damage though. Nothing like the judge was dealing with beneath him.

Third in line was Rink. He still held the front of the lawyer's shirt balled in one hand. The other was cocked mid-air by his shoulder, knuckles stained with blood.

On the ground beside them were the two sisters. Neither appeared to be moving.

It looked like they'd tried to get involved when things went down. It hadn't ended well for them.

Drake sat and stared back at the Sheriff. Paused a few moments, then raised his hands by his side.

The Sheriff just shook his head and dropped his arm to the ground, lowered the rest of himself flat onto his back.

"You boys alright?" Drake asked.

"Good," Kade said. He stood to full height, left the judge beneath him.

Ajax and Rink did the same.

Drake rose onto his right palm and pulled his feet up beneath him. He kept his left hand pressed into his stomach, stood and went to Ava's side.

A whole new flood of anger passed through him as he checked for a pulse. Found it. Used his right hand to untie her bindings.

He stared at the hideous damage Notch had done to her leg, sensed his friends approach from behind him.

"She okay?" Ajax asked.

"No," Drake said. "She won't die, but she's in a world of hurt."

"How bout you?"

Drake twisted his head side to side. "I'll live."

The fake Beth walked over from the wall. She hugged the drop cloth tight around her and sniffed loudly.

Said nothing.

"What happens here now?" Kade asked.

"Good question," Drake said and turned to look at the Sheriff. None of the four men had moved. "Sheriff?"

Sheriff Spore raised his left hand and twirled it in a circular motion. "I've got this. You guys get out of here. Get her to a hospital."

Drake raised Ava's shoulders up from the table with his right arm and slid it beneath her. He winced as he pushed the broken stub of his left hand behind her knees and lifted her into the air with a grunt.

"Yo, we can take her," Ajax said.

Drake again shook his head. "This one's on me. I got her."

He started for the door.

"Can one of you call Sage at Saint Mike's and tell her we're en route?"

"On it," Kade said.

"I'll go get the truck," Rink said. He hooked an arm around fake Beth and took off at a quick walk. Together they disappeared outside.

Drake rested the back of his arms against the table for a moment to let Rink get a head start and give Kade a second to call Sage. He then hefted Ava up and walked past the eight dead or broken individuals lying scattered around the barn into the night.

Ajax on one side of him, Kade on the other.

The original Zoo Crew.

Chapter Sixty-One

Drake pulled his shoulder bag from the front seat of his truck, reached across his body and unlatched the truck door. Climbed out and headed towards the law school.

He looked down at the monstrosity of a cast that now engulfed his left hand and shook his head in disgust.

When they'd gotten to the hospital the night before, Sage had everything arranged. Two nurses were ready and waiting with a wheelchair to take Ava straight to x-ray.

An hour later she was in surgery.

Once Drake got Ava loaded into the wheelchair, it took Sage about ten seconds to sniff out his broken hand. She knew better than to even suggest a wheelchair for him.

Still, she walked him to x-ray herself and fussed over him like a mother hen the entire time. Even applied the cast herself.

Drake was sure she had work she should be doing elsewhere, even pointed it out to her. Repeatedly.

She wouldn't hear of it. Eventually told him to shut up and do as he was told.

Now twelve hours later, the full scope of what she'd done to him was setting in. His hand was useless. He kept jabbing himself with the cast.

Even poor Suzy Q had gotten an unintentional whack from it.

Drake slid in through the side door to the law school wearing a long sleeve pullover with the sleeves down as far as they would extend. They managed to cover most of it, everything except the top few inches around the palm of his hand.

Bright white against tan skin.

For midday midweek the halls were empty. Drake stuck to the back stairwell and nodded a couple quick hellos. Put out the vibe that it was not a day to stop and talk.

It worked.

Until he got to the clinic office.

He wasn't intending to stay long. Just grab his laptop and a few books. He did, after all, have a brief to get written and he needed to get on it as soon as he could.

Typing with a broken hand was not going to be an enjoyable experience.

Greg and Wyatt were both sitting at their desks as he walked in, both with their backs to him.

Drake hoped to slip in and out undetected. He went straight to his desk and gathered his things, turned to find both of them facing him.

"You weren't *really* trying to sneak out like that were you?" Wyatt asked.

"I mean, you're good, but it's not like you're a damn ninja or something," Greg added.

Drake smiled. Shook his head. Said nothing.

Greg started to fire another jab but stopped himself short. His eyes bulged at the cast on Drake's hand.

"Holy shit, it's true isn't it?"

Drake raised his hand and looked down at the cast. "What?"

"All of it," Wyatt said. "The whole school's been abuzz this morning."

"Yeah, about how you kicked Lauer's ass, stormed a child trafficking ring," Greg said.

"Saved Ava's life," Wyatt added.

Drake rolled his eyes. "You guys shouldn't believe everything you hear."

Twelve hours and the stories had already taken on mythical proportions.

Worse yet, they weren't *that* far off. The fact that even that much had gotten out surprised him.

It hadn't come from the Crew. One of the others? One of the girls maybe?

"Oh, come on," Greg said. "Give us something here."

"What are you guys, journalists?" Drake asked.

He made no effort to hide his annoyance. He really wasn't upset at their asking. He'd expected that.

For some reason he didn't feel quite right discussing it. Not until everything got straightened out. It didn't feel like his story to tell.

"Nothing?" Wyatt asked. He looked hurt.

"Cover to cover exclusive," Drake said. "But not right now."

Thought a moment longer and held up his hand. "They gave me morphine. Details are still a little fuzzy."

They hadn't given him anything. Sage tried. He wouldn't let her. He'd wanted his mind sharp in case anything else occurred during the night.

Both his friends stared at him warily, trying to use silence to make him crack.

After a while they gave up and shifted their gaze to the door.

Drake followed their look to see Lauer standing there. His stomach dropped, tongue feeling three sizes too large for his dry mouth.

He knew he was going to have to face Lauer soon enough. Hated like hell that it was happening already.

From the look on Lauer's face, he felt the same way.

"Could you guys give us a few minutes?" Drake asked. He turned his head towards Greg and Wyatt, but kept his eyes on Lauer.

Neither one moved.

Drake wrestled a crumpled five dollar bill from his pocket and tossed it onto Greg's lap. "Have a soda on me."

Slowly, reluctantly, both rose and departed. Left Drake and Lauer standing alone in the office.

For several seconds, neither one spoke. Or even blinked.

"Listen, professor," Drake began. His voice was raspy. No hint of a shake or crack though. "I can't begin to tell you how sorry I am."

Lauer walked past him and placed his bag atop the desk. He turned and sat beside it, his short legs swinging several inches above the floor.

"I know what we, what I, did was an enormous offense. I understand entirely if you press charges, or if you have me removed from school."

Lauer kept his eyes focused on the ground, seeming to debate something internally. "Is she okay?"

Drake breathed for the first time since Lauer walked in.

"She will be. Her left leg is shattered. They put in two rods and a bunch of screws this morning. She has a couple of toes that will be permanently disfigured."

"Hmm," Lauer said, his eyes still averted. "And you?"

Without thinking, Drake lifted the cast. "Broken hand. It'll heal."

"And the girls?"

"All alive and accounted for."

Lauer shifted his eyes from the floor to Drake. He kept his voice low and even, traces of shame, guilt, humiliation, anger, all mixed in.

"I don't want you to think I condone what happened, because I don't. We are lawyers. We don't participate in vigilante, cowboy shit like that.

"Entering this profession means submitting yourself to the greater judicial system. To accepting that we are part of a whole, and that none of us can circumvent that whole if and when we choose."

Drake nodded, waited for the hammer to come down on him.

"After you left last night, I sat out on the porch for a long time. Thought about what you did. What might happen to Ava, to those girls.

"About the situation that wouldn't have even existed if I'd had the courage to stop it years ago."

Drake raised his eyes, focused on Lauer.

"Make no mistake. This will be the only time we ever speak of this. And it will damned sure be the only break I cut you. You're on paper thin ice moving forward."

Drake waited for him to continue. Nothing more was said.

"But we're good?" Drake asked.

"We're good. Now get the hell out of here. I don't want to see you again until at least Monday."

Drake left without another word.

Chapter Sixty-Two

"Good afternoon Mr. Bell, I don't believe we've met. My name is Darcy."

The receptionist at the District Attorney's office extended her hand across the desk to Drake and gave her best impression of a warm smile. She tried not to let him see her wince as he shook her hand.

Drake smirked, made sure she saw it.

"Good to meet you."

Drake delivered it in a monotone voice. Flat expression.

The point was received.

Darcy buzzed him past the desk and on into Wise's office without further comment.

Like Darcy, Wise seemed a little too eager to rise and shake his hand. To offer him a seat. Ask if he'd like a cup of coffee.

Drake waved off everything. He knew at the end of the day he needed the DA's office. Also knew that proverbial day was not today.

Opted to be aloof without coming off as outright hostile.

"Thank you for coming in to see me on such short notice," Wise said as he shuffled a stack of papers in front of him.

"Thanks for calling," Drake said. "I assume the Sheriff contacted you?"

"He did," Wise said. He located what he was looking for and dropped it down in front of him. "Called to tell me that as of this morning Mayor Maria Sloan and a Yelena Gulov have been placed under arrest. They are being held for kidnapping, human trafficking, maiming and two counts of accessory to murder."

Drake nodded. That pretty much matched the list he'd been working on in his head.

"Those are the only two arrests?"

Wise leaned back and assumed his standard position with fingers locked across his stomach. Sighed. "Patricia Harken, Riley Bennett, Judge Minot Tanner, and Dr. Brice Schievers have all been instructed not to leave Missoula County."

Drake's eyes narrowed. He could sense there was more coming, something Wise was trying to avoid mentioning.

"What about Sheriff Spore?"

"What about him?" Wise asked.

Drake tried to read the man across from him. To determine if he was being elusive or didn't know what Drake meant.

It appeared to be the latter.

Drake let it go for the time being. "Why aren't they being held as well?"

Wise frowned and sighed again. "They have asked for, and the sheriff has recommended, leniency in exchange for full cooperation."

Bile rose in the back of Drake's throat. He could imagine what Ava's reaction would be if she were sitting here.

Still, he maintained a face that revealed nothing.

"Leniency?"

"They will be given community service. Placed on probation. Fined. The charges will stay off their records."

"Those sound like slaps on the wrist considering the charges you rattled off. The kinds of punishment handed out for misdemeanors, not criminal offenses."

Wise kept his fingers interlocked. He leaned forward and rested his elbows on the desk. "You have to understand, right now the mayor is sitting in county lockup, going to prison for a very long time. This is not the time to try and wipe out a large chunk of the Missoula County aristocracy."

It was everything Drake could do to keep from flying across the desk. From using the new club on his left hand to make Wise's face look like Ava's toes.

Still, he maintained his composure.

"Is this still about the upcoming election?"

Wise's frown deepened. "It's complicated."

"Hmm," Drake said and thought about their exchange.

It was clear he hadn't been called in for a social visit. He wasn't even called here out of professional courtesy. Despite the fact that he had tried to involve the DA's office, they had no reason to extend him the same.

"So why am I here right now?"

Wise leveled his eyes on Drake. "They also want the civil suit dropped."

Drake smirked. Twice. "The same civil suit you told me to file?"

"The same civil suit I'm advising you now to drop."

"Advising me?" Drake asked. "On what authority?"

"As a representative of the United States District Attorney's Office."

Drake smirked again, found it amusing that the man who just a day before wouldn't even listen to him now wanted to use the weight of the office to quash him. He rose to leave.

"You know, this is a very small town," Wise said. "And you're not even out of the starting blocks on your career."

The implication, again, was clear.

Drake went for the door and rested a hand on the frame, turned to the look at Wise behind his desk.

"Right now, my partner is lying in a hospital bed across town. As much as I can tell you'd like an answer, I'm not at liberty to give one.

"What I can tell you is this. You're right. It is a very small town. And whether it happens in civil court, or the court of public opinion, we'll make sure you are all crucified for this."

Chapter Sixty-Three

Drake could hear voices long before he arrived.

They sounded heated. At the very least animated.

It was hard to be sure though. Drake didn't speak a word of Spanish.

Every impulse in his body told him to stay far away and let this conversation run its course. Still, he had news to share, and he thought Ava might appreciate a break.

He didn't have to knock and damned sure didn't make the fatal mistake of clearing his throat. He just stepped into the doorway and let his wide shoulders throw a shadow over the light pouring into the room.

Both women stopped speaking at once and turned to look at him.

From the bed, Ava offered a forlorn smile.

From the chair beside it, a woman that looked like Ava in thirty years just stared.

"I'm sorry, I didn't mean to interrupt," Drake said.

"No, it's okay," Ava said. "Mama, this is Drake."

Drake stepped into the room and extended a hand to her. "Pleasure to meet Ms. Zargoza."

She returned the shake. Very limp. Cold eyes stared at him. "I'm sure," she said. She made no effort to hide the contempt in her stare.

"You were just saying you'd like a cup of coffee, right?" Ava asked.

Her mother nodded. Stood. Circled around Drake, paused just past him and turned her chin to her shoulder. "Thank you for rescuing my daughter."

She didn't wait for a reply before stomping out of the room, heeled shoes clicking against the tile.

Drake waited for the sound of them to fall away, then walked around to the right side of the bed.

On the left, Ava's leg was suspended by a sling hanging down from the ceiling. A heavy cast covered everything from her knee to mid-foot. Thick gauze wrap enveloped her toes.

"You'll have to forgive her," Ava said. "She was even less thrilled about me coming to Montana than I was."

"I find that hard to believe."

Ava managed a half smile. Dark circles belied both eyes. Her usual glossy, coiffed hair was in a messy bun atop her head. Designer clothes were replaced with a baggy hospital gown.

It was the most real Drake had ever seen her look.

"How you feeling?" Drake asked.

"Like a pendulum," Ava said. "They'll pump me full of drugs, I fly high for awhile. Fall asleep for an hour or two. Then they wear off and the pain comes rushing back."

Drake looked at her leg again and imagined what it had looked like the night before. The way it flopped about as he carried her to the truck.

"Ava, I am so, so sorry. For everything."

Ava rolled her head to the left against her pillow and looked at her leg suspended above her.

"Yeah, I don't suppose I'm going to be doing much salsa dancing for awhile am I?"

Drake snorted. "I imagine even with that thing on you're better than most of the people in Missoula."

"If by most you mean all, then yes."

A pair of matching half-smiles crossed their faces.

"Besides, I'm guessing you'll be on the first plane to Baton Rouge as soon as you're fit to travel?"

The smile faded from Ava's face. "There's still nothing there but a pile of rubble. Why would I go back?"

Drake was unable to hide the surprise on his face. "You hate it here. I can't imagine this helps much." He made a gesture to the door. "And based on..."

He let his voice trail off. No need to spell it out for her.

"That's why we were arguing," Ava said. "She wants to drive me out of here this weekend. I told her I intend to stay."

Drake pulled the chair up closer beside the bed. He rested his wrists on the edge of the mattress and lowered himself into it.

His gaze focused on the opposite wall.

"You look sad," Ava said.

"No, not at all," Drake said. "Just, surprised, is all."

"That's what mama said too. I told her I'm no quitter."

"I don't think anyone would call you a quitter if you left," Drake said. "Besides, it wasn't your idea to be here anyway."

"Hmm," Ava said, rolled her head to stare out the door. "She's a very nice lady. This whole thing is just hard for her right now."

"I took no offense. I can't even imagine."

Ava pulled her eyes from the door, back to Drake. "I hear you saved my life."

Drake made a face. "It was my fault you were there to begin with."

"Don't do that," Ava said. "I'm a big girl. I wanted in on this case. There was nothing you could have done."

Drake kept his eyes averted, tried his best to mask the guilt he felt. "Who told you that anyway?"

"Sage stopped by a little bit ago. How's your hand?"

Drake held up the cast for her to see. "I'll live."

Ava reached over with her right hand and folded it atop his. Gripped half cast and half flesh.

Neither one spoke for a long moment.

"I just came from the DA's office," Drake said.

"And?"

"They only plan to prosecute the mayor and her sister."

"What?"

Drake paused, realized the question wasn't one of disbelief. She really had no idea what he was talking about.

"There's a lot you missed," he said. "I'll fill you in when you're feeling better."

The half smile returned. "Thank you. What about our civil suit?"

Drake smirked. "They want us to drop it."

The smile faded. Her eyes bulged a bit. "What did you tell them?"

"I told them I'd have to talk to my partner."

Ava looked him in the face. Arched an eyebrow. "Anything else?"

Drake stared back at her. Eventually his face cracked into a smile. A small chuckle followed.

"I told them to go to hell."

Chapter Sixty-Four

Drake had one last visit to make.

This time the voices he heard were softer. Sounded much more pleasant. Were spoken in a language he understood.

Drake ducked just inside the door and wrapped against it with the back of his knuckles.

Beth and Ella both looked up at him. Smiled.

Beth was seated in the bed, the back of it inclined to forty-five degrees. She wore a light pink cardigan over her hospital gown and an enormous smile.

Ella sat beside her in a chair. Her feet were propped on a corner of the bed. Many of the bandages had been removed from her face and hands.

"Hello, hello," Drake said as he stepped inside.

"Hey there," Ella said.

"Hello yourself," Beth replied.

"So tomorrow's the big day huh?" Drake asked.

Beth rubbed her stomach. Gave a nervous smile. "Tomorrow morning."

"Good for you," Drake said. "We'll all be here when you come out. Help you welcome the little...?"

He twisted his head to the side, gave an expression that relayed his uncertainty.

"Girl," Beth finished for him. "I'm having a little girl."

"A little girl," Drake echoed.

"And I'm keeping her," Beth said. "After everything that's happened, there's no way I'm giving her up."

Drake's eyebrows raised. A surprised smile crossed his face. "Wow. Congratulations. To both of you."

Both women smiled, blushed a bit.

"Also, I was going to wait until tomorrow to tell you, but now works too," Beth said. "I'm going to name her Annabell."

"Annabell," Drake repeated. "Very...Southern. I like it."

"My mother's name was Anna. And your last name is Bell, so..."

Drake's jaw dropped open. "You didn't...I mean..."

Beth smiled, waved a hand at him. "There's no way I could ever repay you for what you've done. This was the least I could do."

"Yeah, but still..."

Beth cut him off. "And there just wasn't a whole lot I could do with Drake."

Drake broke into a laugh. Shook his head. "No, I don't suppose there is. Thank you, and you're welcome."

Amiable silence settled over the room for a moment.

"You guys going to stick around here?" Drake asked.

"Well, we were just talking about that," Ella said.

"Now that I won't be getting the money for carrying the baby, we're not real sure," Beth added.

Ella reached over and took Beth's hand. "We'll figure it out together though."

"Well, I might be able to help with that," Drake said. "Last week, Ava and I filed that civil suit on your behalf. It's scheduled for a preliminary hearing in a couple of weeks."

"Meaning?" Beth asked.

"Well, now that we know who all was involved," Drake began, "to quote Ava, it means you're going to get paid."

Both girls smiled.

"What about the others?" Beth asked.

"They're still at the Hawthorne now. I was going to talk to them tomorrow. See if they wanted to be named as parties or not."

Beth laid her head against the pillow. Her eyes glistened beneath the overhead lights.

"Thank you. Thank you so much."

"My pleasure."

Beth paused a moment, took a deep breath.

"You're going to keep this up and I'm going to have to name the poor child Drake after all, aren't I?"

Epilogue

Drake sent the text message before stopping to see Beth. He didn't know how long he'd be in with her, but he sent it anyway.

Figured he could wait around if need be.

As was, he timed it just about right.

Drake stayed with Beth and Ella until a nurse informed him visiting hours were over. He gave Ella a hug and kissed Beth atop her head.

Told them both he'd see them in the morning.

He found Sage just as she was exiting the operating suite. She looked very tired, but was smiling just the same.

"I was wondering if you'd remember," she said. No formal greeting at all.

Drake feigned being hurt. Made a face. "Come on now. It's Wednesday. Have I ever let you down?"

Sage offered another sleepy smile and drifted over so her shoulder bumped into him. Said nothing.

Drake looped an arm around her. She slid a hand around his waist.

"Thanks for looking out for me last night," Drake said.

Sage ignored the comment. "How's it feeling?"

"Eh," Drake said. "The cast itself is worse than the pain."

"Just wait until it starts itching," Sage said.

Drake snorted. He'd already encountered that once today. A fate worse than hell.

Together the two of them wound their way to the cafeteria. Enjoyed the easy silence of being together.

The hospital hallways were barren as they made the familiar walk to the cafeteria. Most of the staff was already gone for the day. Very few visitors ever went into the back halls.

A few nurses looked at the pair of them and smiled. An orderly nodded hello.

"So, sadly, no Firetower tonight," Drake said. He dropped his arm from Sage's shoulder and pulled open the door.

"Damn," Sage said. "I had my heart set on it too."

"I ordered in something else though," Drake said. "Hopefully that'll work."

Sage made an inquisitive face and stepped through. She smiled as she saw Ajax and Kade sitting at a table along the far window.

A stack of sandwiches sat between them. An order of wings for Ajax.

"Oh, dinner and a show," Sage said. "How'd you manage to pull this one off?"

"I promised to buy them dinner," Drake said.

They shared a laugh and went to join their friends along the back wall. They offered hugs for Sage, fist bumps for Drake.

Conversation was light for the first few minutes. It had been a long day. A long *couple* of days. They all ate ravenously.

When nothing remained of the food but a vapor trail, all four settled back into their seats.

Kade burped. Ajax looped an arm over his back rest. Drake fought the urge to loosen his belt.

"So, to what do we owe the pleasure of dinner?" Sage asked.

"Courtesy of the world's greatest tightwad no less?" Ajax added.

Drake smiled, didn't try to refute the statement.

It wasn't wrong.

"Just my way of saying thank you," he said.

Sage offered a polite half smile. Ajax rolled his eyes.

Kade waved a hand back and forth in front of him. "No no no. None of that. We're not going to have you acting like you owe us because of all this or something."

"That's not how we roll," Ajax added.

Drake pursed his lips, tilted his head and weighed their words. "I'm not thanking you for helping with this. I mean, thanks, I do appreciate it, but that's not what this was about."

Ajax and Kade both stared at him. Sage made a motioning gesture with her hand.

"This summer..." Drake started, but thought better of it. Instead he decided to cut straight to the chase. "It's good to be back. With family."

Sage smiled. Ajax and Kade both nodded.

Drake didn't elaborate further. He didn't have to. They all got the message.

Comfortable silence again fell over the group.

Kade picked some melted cheese from his sandwich foil. Ajax slurped on the last of a soda. Sage checked her watch, begrudgingly rose to leave.

"So I was thinking," she said. "Maybe hit the Flats in the morning? We did miss today."

"I was thinking the same thing," Drake said. "I'm just wondering how that'll go dragging this thing around. Not supposed to get it wet, right Nurse Keuhl?"

"Not unless you want to cut it off and start all over again," she said. "You could always just wrap a plastic bag around it."

"I'll figure something out," Drake said.

"I heard on the radio this morning they're calling for the first dusting up at Snow Bowl this weekend," Kade said. "Won't be long and we'll be trading fishing rods for ski poles."

"Your hand be ready in time?" Ajax asked, nodded towards the cast on Drake's arm.

"I'll figure something out," Drake said again.

Made in the USA
San Bernardino, CA
22 April 2018